passion and affect

ALSO BY LAURIE COLWIN

passion
and affect

LAURIE COLWIN

HarperPerennial
A Division of HarperCollins*Publishers*

Acknowledgments:

"The Big Plum" and "Dangerous French Mistress" originally appeared in *Antaeus*; "Smartest Woman in America" originally appeared in *Audience*; "A Road in Indiana" originally appeared in *Cosmopolitan*; "The Elite Viewer" originally appeared in *Mademoiselle*; "Animal Behavior," "The Man Who Jumped into the Water," and "Mr. Parker" originally appeared in *The New Yorker*; "The Girl With the Harlequin Glasses" and "The Water Rats" (under the title "Man With a Gun") originally appeared in *Redbook*.

This book was originally published in 1974 by Viking Press. It is here reprinted by arrangement with Viking Press.

HarperCollins books may be purchased for educational, business, or sales promotional use. For information please write: Special Markets Department, HarperCollins Publishers, Inc., 10 East 53rd Street, New York, NY 10022.

First HarperPerennial edition published 1995.

Library of Congress Cataloging-in-Publication Data

Colwin, Laurie.
    Passion and affect / Laurie Colwin. — 1st ed.
       p.   cm.
   ISBN 0-06-097633-0
   1. United States—Social life and customs—20th century—Fiction. I. Title.
PS3553.04783P3 1995
813′.54—dc20   94-24623

95 96 97 98 99 RRD 10 9 8 7 6 5 4 3 2 1

TO MY PARENTS AND TO JOHN SERBER

passion   a state of desire or emotion that represents the influence of what is external and opposes thought and reason as the true activity of the human mind

—Webster's Third New International Dictionary

af'fect   (L. *affectus,* from *afficere,* to apply oneself to.) psy: the emotional reactions associated with an experience

—Cyclopedic Medical Dictionary

contents

passion and affect

# animal behavior

Nothing is more easy than to tame an animal and few things are more difficult than to get it to breed freely in confinement, even in the many cases when the male and female unite.

—Charles Darwin, *The Origin of Species*

O<small>N THE ROOF</small> of the East Wing of the American Naturalist Museum was a greenhouse, blocked from public view by turrets and façades. The skylights could be opened with a brass pole. Every third pane was a window. In midmorning, and sometimes in the afternoon, Roddy Phelps went up the spiral staircase to the finch room of the greenhouse and took a nap.

It was the middle of March, and Roddy was feeling slightly but constantly chilled. The weather made no sense to his body, although he knew it was supposed to be cold before the beginning of spring. Even on the coldest, rainiest days, the greenhouse was warm and faintly tropic. Birdcages were arranged on rows of pine tables, and on an empty table in the farthest row, by the window, Roddy took his naps. He had stashed a car pillow under a shelf in a paper bag.

The greenhouse was filled with potted ferns, palms, and heather. Ivy hung from crossbeams in mossy wire baskets. Each species of bird had its own room. Drifting off to sleep, Roddy was soothed by the diminutive, random noises the birds made—twitters, clacks, and cheeps, which he thought of as auditory litter. Once in a while, he brought a transistor radio with him and listened to the birds counterpointing Mozart.

3

The year before, Roddy's wife, Garlin, had left him, taking their child, Sara Justina, and retired to the country. At Thanksgiving, New Year's, and Easter, Roddy drove to Templeton, New Hampshire, and collected Sara Justina, who spent these holidays and a part of the summer with Roddy and his parents in Westchester. The rest of the time, silence was generally maintained between New York and Templeton, except for legal occasions when separation, alimony, divorce, and child-support papers passed between Roddy and Garlin. These entailed long conversations with the lawyers for both sides, and expensive, jagged long-distance calls from New York to New Hampshire.

The last week in March there was a brief hot spell, and Roddy's chill became more acute. Dampness settled in his bones. He began to think that he was suffering from eyestrain and spent dizzy, unfocused, and dislocated days feeling as if he were hung over. The naps in the finch room sometimes helped, but often they made his unfocused condition worse and he staggered off the table while the room went black, yellow, and dazzling gray in front of his eyes.

After Garlin's departure, Roddy had gone into a work spurt that produced two papers on the social behavior of caged finches —one for *Scientific American* and one for *American Birds*. The uncorrected galleys of both had been lying on his desk for several months. Then he started on the breeding and nesting patterns of the African finch in captivity. He had been studying this aspect of the finch since December but had run into trouble, as his finches seemed unwilling to breed in their large Victorian cages and appeared uninterested in building nests out of the pampas grass, string, and clover he provided for them.

Roddy had a corner office on the sixth floor of the museum, which housed the Department of Animal Behavior. He kept two pairs of finches there—Aggie and Bert, Gem and Russell— pets, not experimental birds, who had been left by a colleague departing for the Galápagos. When Roddy arrived in the morning, he let them out of their cage, and in the evening he spent an hour getting them back in.

The finch room was his exclusively. There was a greenhouse

caretaker, José Jacinto Flores, whose job it was to clean the cages and feed the birds, but, by friendly edict, in the finch room Roddy took care of this himself. José Jacinto had appropriated a back room where he kept a tank of tropical fish and a pair of lovebirds who warbled tenderly to each other. He was a wiry, squat man, the color of cherry wood, and Roddy often saw him smoking a cheroot with the windows open, speaking softly in Spanish to his birds.

The table Roddy napped on was the last in a series of four. He was blocked by cages of birds and pots of palm and heather that shut him off from view, he thought, since he could never see anything through them.

On the last Thursday in March, Roddy left his office and went up to the greenhouse. He had not slept well the night before, tossing and brooding about his experiments, settling finally into a brief, unrefreshing sleep. A few minutes before in his office, the telephone rang and it was Garlin to tell him that Sara Justina had bronchitis.

"Did you call just to tell me that?" Roddy asked. Garlin almost never called him when Sara Justina was sick.

"Bronchitis isn't a cold," said Garlin.

"What am I supposed to do? Do you want me to come up to Templeton?"

"I thought you should know she's sick, and, by the way, did your lawyer call mine about the final papers?"

"I have to check," said Roddy.

"It's your life," Garlin said.

"What's that supposed to mean?"

"It means that you should have checked a month ago. You have no idea what's serious and what isn't. Your marriage is being disbanded and you haven't even bothered to call your lawyer."

"I've been working very hard, Garlin, and I think this whole thing is unpleasant enough without remarks like that."

"That's why your marriage is being disbanded," said Garlin, and she hung up.

The finches peered from the curtain rod. Aggie, his favorite, flew down and sat on his dictionary. Roddy watched her, feeling tired and worn down, like a statue battered by the weather. In the dove room he noticed it was raining. The sky was silvery, and drops hit the glass on a slant. At the entrance to the finch room, chilled and desperate for his nap, he discovered a girl standing in front of one of the cages. She had some millet seed on the tips of her fingers and was waiting patiently for one of the birds to take it from her.

"What are you doing here?" Roddy said.

The girl didn't move her hand but turned to look at him. She was a small girl in a gray lab coat, whose thick, ashy hair was loosely knotted at her neck. She had an oval, symmetrical face and eyes that were an intense, almost colorless gray. Under the lab coat she was wearing a gray skirt, sweater, and brown stockings.

"I'm sorry," she said. "'Are these your birds?"

"Yes, and I'd like to know what you're doing here."

"I'm awfully sorry. I'm down on the fifth floor with Dr. Reddicker, working on song patterns. Until yesterday I didn't even know there was a greenhouse here, so I just came up to see what it was like. Sorry."

"Are you new here?" Roddy said.

"I started a couple of months ago. I'm Dr. Reddicker's assistant, in the doctoral program."

"After you've been here a while, you get hysterical about security."

The first three floors of the museum were open to the public and contained, in addition to cases of stuffed birds in replicas of their natural habitats, a bookstore, a small but rare gem collection, the letters and papers of John James Audubon, and several galleries filled with paintings, drawings, sculpture, and tapestries of birds. It was the largest and best collection of its kind in the world. The rest of the museum was devoted to research and teaching facilities, and rigid security was maintained. All members of the staff, from the ornithologists and researchers to the girls in the bookstore, wore plastic tags bearing their names and color photographs. Roddy stepped closer to the girl. Her tag read "Mary

Leibnitz," and the photograph looked as if it had taken her by
surprise. Roddy's tag was pinned to his jacket in his office.

"I'm Raiford Phelps," he said.

"This tag embarrasses me," Mary Leibnitz said. "Everyone
knows my name before I'm introduced."

"Do you want to be shown around?" Roddy asked. She nodded,
and he steered her through the parrot room, the sicklebills, wood-
peckers, and hummingbirds. He led her back through the finches,
canaries, and doves.

She stopped before a cage of pigeons. "I love the sound they
make," she said. "It's kind of a gurgle. I've tried to imitate it, but
I can't. Thanks very much for showing me through."

He watched her as she walked toward the stairs. She had a serious kind of grace, as if she alone were responsible for holding
herself together. Roddy got his pillow from the shelf, took off his
shoes, and lay down on the pine table. He leaned down to turn on
his radio, but the thought of music suddenly upset him. The
finches chirped him into sleep.

It became colder and less springlike. There were
days when Roddy could barely keep his eyes open. He began to
take two naps—one in the morning and one in the afternoon. He
paced in his office, skimmed his galleys, went to bed early, twist-
ing, brooding, unable to sleep. He made several trips to the fifth
floor to look for Mary Leibnitz. He met her once briefly in the
hallway and told her that if she came to his office he would show
her what he was working on. Walking past her office one day, he
saw her sitting diminutively next to Ethel Reddicker, a large red-
headed woman, going over a series of charts. A week went by and
Mary Leibnitz did not appear at his office.

Every Sunday night, Roddy called Templeton to speak to Sara
Justina, with whom he had long baby conversations, followed by
terse, practical conversations with Garlin. Mondays he awoke feeling drained. It seemed that on Monday it always rained or was
overcast. He began to oversleep in the finch room, and he brought
an alarm clock with him.

One Monday he forgot to set it and woke to find Mary Leibnitz standing by a cage looking at him; he blinked to get the blackness out of the room and blinked again because he was horrified. Nothing that fought its way to his voice was appropriate. He merely stared at her.

She looked at him calmly—he might have been one of the birds she waited to feed. Her lab coat hung away from her. She turned and walked out.

"Wait," Roddy said.

Mary Leibnitz stopped next to a cage of green siskins.

He got off the table, stepped into his shoes, and confronted her. "I don't like this," he said. "Being spied on."

"I'm not spying on you," Mary said. "I went to your office, but you weren't there, so I thought I might find you up here."

"I *told* you to come to my office."

"I did, but you weren't there. I'm really awfully sorry, but I don't know why you're making such a fuss."

"I'm not making a fuss," Roddy said. "I just don't like being spied on."

"What you mean is that you take secret naps up here and you don't like being caught out. There's nothing wrong with it. I'd sleep up here too. It smells good."

"That's not why. I don't like my privacy invaded."

"Would it interest you to know I've seen you sleeping before?"

"Well, I don't like it. I don't like it at all. What are you doing, snooping around up here?"

Mary put a cool hand on his arm. "Don't shout," she said. "You're overreacting. I've been here a couple of times to talk to Mr. Flores. He's Peruvian, and I used to live in Lima when I was little, so I come up to speak Spanish to him."

"How nice for you."

"No need to be nasty," Mary said. "I really *am* sorry I woke you up. Goodbye."

"How long were you standing around?"

"You lost ten minutes of privacy," Mary said. "I didn't wake you, because you looked so angelic." She moved as quickly as a cat and was gone before Roddy had collected himself.

On Saturday afternoon, Roddy was going over galleys in his office at the museum. He heard a knock and turned to find Mary Leibnitz standing at the threshold, wearing bluejeans and her lab coat.

"Hello," she said. "Should I go away? I only came by because I wanted to go upstairs and was checking to see if you were here."

"Why did you ask if you should go away?"

"You said you didn't want your privacy invaded. I don't want to people your solitude unless you want it peopled."

"People my solitude," Roddy repeated. She looked very fragile in the doorway. There was a sweetness in her eyes when she looked at him.

"Can I go up and see the finches? I mean, is it all right?" she asked.

Roddy stood looking at Mary for a long time before he spoke. "You're not like other people," he said.

Mary looked at the floor. "Can I go up?"

"I'll go with you," said Roddy, and he took her arm.

She followed him up the spiral staircase. He was tall and rangy and hunched his shoulders. Where his hair waved slightly, it was reddish, but generally it was brown. By a cage of golden finches, Mary studied him. He had round green eyes, with delicate lines around them that made him look tired in an exquisite way. His skin was very fine and his nose was flat. In the light he looked boyish.

"What do you want to see?" he asked.

"I just wanted to be here," Mary said. "I don't think I've ever seen a room I've liked so much."

"There's a lot I can show you," Roddy said.

"I just wanted to be here," Mary said. She smiled, then she stopped. "It never occurred to me. I'm really sorry. I probably took you away from your work, just for an aesthetic thrill. I mean,

I didn't want to come up for any scientific reason. I'm really sorry if I took your time."

"It's all right," said Roddy. "At least you like birds."

When they opened the door of his office, Aggie, Bert, Russell, and Gem started from the curtain rod and flew to the bookshelves. Roddy pulled down the blinds.

"I have to get them into their cage. Stand by the switch, and when I tell you, turn the lights off." He stood in the center of the room, waving his arms. The birds left the bookshelves and flew to the corners. "Now!" he shouted.

Mary turned off the lights and heard the sound of wings threshing the air, then beating furiously against the wall.

"O.K.," Roddy said. "Put them on." He had a towel in his hand and from it poked a tiny white-and-yellow head. "It's Aggie," he said. "Come and see."

Mary watched as he put the towel to the cage door and Aggie hopped out to the back of the cage, looking rumpled and frightened. "Can't you catch them any other way?" she asked.

"No. I go through this every afternoon."

"I can't bear to hear them beating against the wall like that," Mary said.

"There isn't any other way. They have to be in their cage at night."

"Won't they fly onto your hand?"

"Not these. They're friendly but not very trusting."

"Mr. Flores seems to pick them out of the air."

"You stick with Flores," Roddy said. "He's a regular Francis of Assisi."

When Gem, Russell, and Bert had been caught, Mary leaned back against the wall. "That's the most unnatural sound I've ever heard," she said.

"No more unnatural than anything else you have to get used to," said Roddy, covering the cage with a blue cloth.

They walked away from the museum past a line of trees. Damp leaves printed the sidewalks.

"I live quite close by," Mary said. "Would you like to come and have coffee?"

"I don't think so," Roddy said. "I've got lots of work to do."

Mary lived in a brownstone with a wide oak door. Her apartment looked over a garden in whose center a cement Cupid with a broken-off right arm was standing in a pool of watery dead leaves. The pictures on the wall were old-fashioned watercolors of flowers. She had a small prayer rug and a Peruvian wall hanging. Her furniture was plain and comfortable. There was an oak desk, an oak table, a gray sofa, and two blue armchairs.

From the window Roddy could see the spires of the museum and the edge of the park. In the corner of the garden grew a catalpa tree, whose dried pods hung like snakeskins amid green emerging buds.

Mary appeared and put a tray of coffee and cups on the table.

"It's bliss here," Roddy said. "How can you like the finch room so much if you have this?"

"I'm glad you decided to come up after all," Mary said. "Come have coffee."

"Wait a minute," Roddy said. He took her by the shoulders and pointed her into the afternoon light. Her eyes were level and serious. Then she grinned and he kissed her.

"Thank you," she said.

"Thank me?"

"I was hoping you'd kiss me, but I didn't know how I could arrange it. I'm shy."

"You don't seem very shy," said Roddy.

"I am, but not in usual ways," she said. She bent toward the coffeepot, but he caught her arm and kissed her again. They stood at the window with their hands interlocked, and she scanned his face as if she were memorizing it.

"I'm married," he said.

"You shouldn't have kissed me, then."

"I mean, I'm getting a divorce. I'm in the process of it. I'm not telling you that so you'll think I'm available or anything." He let go of her hand and sat down.

"Raiford," Mary said.

"Roddy," said Roddy.

"Roddy. How old are you?"

"Thirty-one."

"You're very silly for thirty-one."

"I don't like this conversation," said Roddy. He drank his coffee and looked out the window. "You have no idea how nice it is here. Why am I silly for thirty-one?"

"Because first of all you kiss me, then you say you're married, then you say you're not married, and then you tell me not to think you're available. How do you know I'm available? How do you know I'm not married?"

"Are you?" Roddy said. "I saw the picture of that guy on your mantelpiece. Is he someone in your life?"

"He used to be my fiancé," Mary said. "We were going to get married last July, but we broke it off. He's in India now, but we write to each other. We're still friends."

"You are?"

"We started out friends," Mary said. "You can stop being lovers, but you can't cancel out friendship. Maybe it's different if you're getting a divorce—harder to know if you and your wife are still friends."

"I don't know what we were," said Roddy. "We had a kid, but it didn't seem to help much."

Mary looked at him sadly. He was sitting in a dark corner of the sofa; his head was lowered, hidden in a shadow. When she turned a lamp on, he looked up and the glow hit him full in the face. She sat on her side of the sofa watching him. The light played over his face like expression, and when he finally turned to her the slight lines around his eyes softened.

"This is the first time I've felt comfortable in months," Roddy said. "You have no idea how nice you are."

On Sunday evening, Roddy sat in his apartment waiting for Mary, who was coming to borrow his copy of *Darwin's Finches*. He was happy and nervous anticipating her, so he thought about her apartment, which to him was like the finch room. He liked the way she watched him, the serious way she reacted. "It's like a movie, being with you," he had said to her. "I feel like a camera being watched by a camera. It's like being in a situation and outside it at the same time. If I look at you, I can watch me being here. I've never seen anything like it, the way you take note."

She arrived on time, wearing a raincoat, a gray skirt, a white sweater.

"Don't you ever wear anything that's a color?" Roddy asked.

His apartment was on the ground floor of a dingy brick building near the river. In the living room was an aluminum work table, piled with papers, two cheap chairs, and a matching sofa. It looked as if someone had lived in the two rooms for a brief, uninspired time and had fled abruptly, leaving faded furniture and curtains behind. In the middle of the floor was an air-conditioner turned over on its side. Its parts were strewn in a circle around it.

"I'm in the process of fixing it," Roddy explained.

Behind a partition was his bedroom—a nook big enough for a bed, on top of which were stacks of clean laundry and a small generator. In the kitchen was a Bunsen burner and a pegboard hung with hammers, ratchets, wrenches, and drills. On the Formica sideboard was an acid beaker that functioned as coffee-maker. There were two tin plates and two tin cups that he had gotten as a premium for buying the five bottles of soy sauce that were lined up on a shelf next to some empty orange-juice tins. The ice-box emitted a hum, and when Roddy hit it with his forearm the door opened, revealing a container of cottage cheese, a bottle of wine, and a carton of eggs.

"That's my next project, that icebox," Roddy said. "I got the hum out once, but it came back."

He made coffee in the acid beaker. There was powdered milk and sugar he had filched from the museum cafeteria.

"What an odd way to live," Mary said. "You go to all the trouble of making coffee with filter paper and then you don't have any proper milk. These are only temporary quarters to you, aren't they?"

"Proper milk, as you call it, doesn't keep, and since I'm not here all that often, why bother?"

"Then why bother about anything?" Mary said.

"I work most of the time. That's what my time is for."

They drank their coffee side by side on the sofa, holding hands. The icebox began to hum.

"I've got to fix that, but first I have to call Templeton. I've been trying to get Garlin all day. She's never in, or else she's not answering the phone." He dragged the telephone from under the couch and dialed a series of numbers.

"Let me speak to Sara," he said into the receiver. "Is she any better? . . . Hello? S. J., it's Poppa. I hear you got a shot. You didn't cry? Well, I'm very pleased to hear that. I'm sending you a postcard in the mail and I want you to send me one of the pictures you draw at school. O.K.? Ask Mama if she wants to speak to me. . . . Hi. I didn't get the lawyer. I'll call him tomorrow. O.K.? Right." He hung up.

Mary had moved to a corner of the sofa, to keep a distance between herself and the conversation.

"Why are you hiding over there?" Roddy said. "To pay me back for calling my wife? You can call your boyfriend in India if you want."

"Don't tease," said Mary. "How old's your little girl?"

"Four."

"Do you have any pictures of her?"

"I don't have anything around," Roddy said. "Most of my stuff is with my parents in Westchester. I brought a whole bunch of stuff back from New Caledonia once—feathers and nests and bows, carved boats, that sort of thing. After I got married, it was all nicely on display, and Sara got her baby hands on what hadn't disintegrated and tore it apart."

"It's a spare life," Mary said, smiling.

"You can be my possession. I'd put you in a little nook and lay flowers at your feet."

"Don't tease," said Mary.

"I wish I *were* teasing," Roddy said. "God, how glad I am you're here."

He took the wine from the icebox, opened it with a corkscrew, and poured out two water glasses.

"Celebration," he said.

"Cheers," said Mary. "It's the beginning of April."

They stood in happy silence, drinking wine. The icebox hummed.

"Stand over here," Roddy said. "I'm going to fix that damned thing once and for all."

"Don't fix it, Roddy. Talk to me."

"I've got the time now and I might not tomorrow. Besides, I can do both. Hand me that wrench—the smaller one."

He took the wrench and a screwdriver and, after taking off the bottom plate, lay on his back, looking into the motor of the icebox.

"There's a flashlight in that drawer," he said. "Can you shine it right above my head so I can see into this?"

She held it as she was told, flashing the beam from time to time onto his face.

"This machine is an antique," Roddy said. "Why do you keep flashing that into my eyes?"

"To behold you."

Half an hour later, the hum diminished, Roddy got up from the floor and took the flashlight from Mary.

"I shouldn't be doing this," he said.

"Fixing the icebox?"

"Asking you if you'll stay here tonight."

"You know I will," said Mary.

"Why?"

"Because it's the right thing to do."

"Do you always do things for a reason?" he asked.

"Aren't you doing this for a reason?"

"Your coming up to the finch room was an act of vast good fortune for me," Roddy said. "You're the nicest person I think I've ever met. You're the only person I've ever met who seems to be *prepared* for things. Are you prepared for a lot of pain?"

"I have no idea what you're talking about," said Mary. "I don't think you do, either." She rinsed the glasses, happy to feel the water running over her wrists.

Every day, they left the museum together, took walks through the park, and had dinner. During the week, they spent nights at Roddy's, and on the weekends at Mary's. Often in the middle of dinner or a walk, they would stop and look at each other seraphically.

"I've never been this happy," Roddy said.

"Neither have I," said Mary.

"I love walking through time with you," Roddy said frequently.

They read each other's books, talked for hours, and planned to write a paper together on the function of song patterns in caged and wild finches. Roddy was astonished at how long Mary liked to sit over dinner. They talked, and quarreled, and kept regular hours. Each day the leaves got rounder. The cherry trees in the museum garden blossomed. The grass was lusher—wet and slick in the evenings. They did not arrive at the museum together in the mornings.

In the middle of June, they strolled through the park. The earth gave up a cold mist that collected in fuzzy halos under the street lights. The trees had blossomed late and were just shedding their petals, which fell on the grass like spilled paint. They did not walk hand in hand but held themselves in a close orbit, arm against arm. They stopped by a stone wall and studied each other. He had a way of keeping his face in a state of blankness tinged only by worry. When the tightness broke and he smiled, Mary sometimes found herself close to tears. Often he looked at her with a tenderness so intense that she had to force herself to make him laugh in order to break it.

"You are a blessing I don't deserve," Roddy said.

"Shut up."

"When I think that it's only chance that you work at the museum, that you might not have come up to the greenhouse . . ."

"You think it's chance that we're together," Mary said. She walked under a plane tree, out of the light.

"Why are we, then?"

"I don't know about you," said Mary, almost mumbling. "But some people act out of love."

He caught her by the elbow. "Does that mean you love me?"

"That's not your business," Mary said.

"What do you mean, it's not my business?"

"It isn't information you really want," she said. "Don't go trying to get me to say what you don't want to hear."

The summer seemed reluctant to break. By the middle of July it was still cold and wet, and the stone corridors of the museum were damp. The days spun themselves out in solid grayness. On a rainy Friday in August, Roddy and Mary ambled under an umbrella toward Mary's apartment. People on the streets moved in slow motion against the downpour, and the trees moved like underwater flora. The front door to Mary's apartment was swollen with damp and Roddy had to shove it open.

He sprawled on the couch and shut his eyes. Mary sat on the floor pouring coffee.

"Are you sleepy?" she asked. For a couple of weeks, he had been edgy and occasionally sleepless.

"I'm trying to see what this will look like in memory," Roddy said. "We're not living in real time. This isn't real time at all."

"It's real enough for me," said Mary. She looked up to find him still lying there, his hands folded on his chest, his eyes shut, like a knight on a medieval coffin.

"It isn't real. It's pleasurable suspension. Real time has nothing to do with chance. It's loaded with obligations and countercharges and misfires."

She put her cup down and wound her arms around her knees. "Is something going to make this change?" she said. "Is that why you're so restless?"

He sat beside her on the floor and took the pins out of her hair. "You think life goes in a straight line, Mary. This all seems clear and straightforward to you, because that's what you're like, but it isn't that way for me."

"If you mean that you have to go to Westchester with Sara Justina, I knew that a long time ago."

"Look, Mary. What we have now is a little gift wrapped up in time. It'll never be this way again. There are things I have to do that will cut me off from you eventually, and you'll hate me." He wound her hair around his wrist. Then he let go, and she got up and sat in a hard-backed chair, clutching the cane seating until she could feel it imprint her hand. She had been haunted for a month, expecting some dire interruption between them.

"If what you're saying, Roddy, is that we can't be together any more, say it. Don't be such a chicken."

He kneeled in front of the chair. "I'm used to these lovely free days, and I get sick to think what the world is going to do to them."

"Talk straight," Mary said. She collected the coffee cups, and when she reached for the cream pitcher it slipped out of her hand and smashed on the floor. She sat down abruptly, put her head in her hands, and cried for several minutes.

Roddy put his arms around her. He ran his fingers over the tears on her face and drew a little pattern on her cheekbone. "I want to maintain the time we have," he said. "But, Mary, the earth spins on its axis and everything changes. You can't freeze things, not things as delicate as this, and hope they'll survive a thaw."

"I don't know how to fight you on this," Mary said, "when I don't know what I'm fighting."

"Time," said Roddy. "I've never seen a life arranged like yours.

It's organized for a kind of comfort. Mine isn't."

Her eyes were very grave. "You said I was a good arranger," she said. "Time is the easiest thing in the world to arrange."

"I want to be with you," Roddy said into her hair. "But I don't see how. All I see is a messy world nibbling at the corners of this."

"You're not talking about the world. You're talking about yourself. The world is outside us. This is an inside job."

"Look, life has a lot of holes in it. This is going to get worse, not better. That's why all this time was so beautiful—because nothing got in the way of it."

She spoke very slowly. "I didn't want to say this to you, Roddy, but you know I love you. I can't get to the bottom of what's bothering you, but if it's something you have to go through by yourself, I'll stand by you. You go off and take care of Sara Justina, and when that's finished we can sort it out. I don't want to live in unreal time with you."

"You're making this very hard for me," he said.

"I'm trying to make it easy. I'm trying to clear a way for you so you can see us," said Mary. "But don't make me hang too long."

"I'll figure it out," Roddy said wildly. "I'll figure it out."

The first week they were apart, Mary worked on a chart on the song patterns of the thrush. She made tapes of canary songs and wrote them down in musical notation, sitting in her tiny office with a set of headphones clamped to her ears. They blotted out the sound of footsteps, but they did not blot out what she replayed over and over in her mind: Roddy talking to her. When Ethel Reddicker went to lunch or lectures, Mary took off her earphones, locked the door, and wept. She stayed away from Roddy's office, but the thought that he was in the building, walking the corridors, using the elevator, made her feel bonded to him.

At night, she ran their moments together through her mind until, with a sense of loss, she realized that she was thinking in the past tense. There was no one she could talk to—she and Roddy had sealed themselves up, keeping their time to themselves.

Then for a month she kept busy, knowing that he was in Westchester with Sara Justina, but when the month was out she found that she was prone to tears that caught her off guard. She walked through the museum in a glazed and headachy state until she came down with a cold that kept her home for three days, watching the rain clouds low over the spires of the museum.

In the beginning of September, she went to the greenhouse when she was certain Roddy would not be there, to speak to José Jacinto Flores. She found him feeding Roddy's finches. His hand was extended into the cage and the birds perched on his sleeve, picking millet from his palm. He greeted her in soft, courtly Spanish.

"Why are you feeding the finches, Mr. Flores?"

"Because he"—José Jacinto nodded toward the empty table—"went to a conference in Bermuda for two weeks, so I have to take care of them."

This information filled Mary with hope and despair in equal parts: he was back—he had gone away without telling her, but he was away. And how could she hear from him if he was in Bermuda?

Mary knew when he came back—she felt it. Then she saw him in the back of a lecture room as she walked by. He was writing on a blackboard, talking to one of the ornithologists. His shoulders were hunched in the old familiar way. Everything about him was familiar, but she couldn't call to him. She had given him her form of trust, and knew, because he had said so, that he trusted her. If he was waiting, it was for a reason—she had taken him on trust and stood by it. In her memory she heard his soft voice say, "You don't realize that I adore you." She raced to her office in tears.

How they contrived to work in the same building, live in the same neighborhood, and never meet amazed her, but they did. She was not the sort of girl to leave notes in his mailbox or letters taped to his office door. When two months had passed, she realized that he was going to do nothing about her and she was filled with a sense of pain so intense it astonished her.

The last bugs floated lazily on the air currents. The weather was hot and wet, or cold and wet. In Mary's garden, a row of cats sat on the wall, baring their teeth, chattering at the chickadees, making little rattles in the back of their throats.

She had got into the habit of using the public entrance to the museum instead of the staff door. It was the third week of public school, and lines of giggling children patrolled by nervous teachers looped around the stone eagles and spilled down the steps, forming rows on the sidewalk.

One morning before she went to her office, Mary stopped in the gem collection, cutting her way through a sea of beings that reached her waist. She looked down on a mat of bobbing heads. There was a mixed din of shouts and giggles, flattened by the stone walls to a loud hush.

The room was packed; she could hardly walk. Children were standing four deep in front of each glass case and a teacher was reading to them about star sapphires from a printed card.

She fled to one of the galleries. A group of quiet children was standing in front of a bronze stork. At the far end of the gallery was a small tapestry behind a glass shield. A brass plaque announced that it had been woven by the nuns of Belley in the sixteenth century. In a lush green field, full of shells and wild flowers, was a heron—pure white and slightly lopsided. Its delicate feet were red, and its wings drooped by its sides. As she walked closer, she saw that on its face was embroidered an expression of almost human mournfulness. The room filled up behind her as she stood. Tears came into her eyes and her mouth twisted. When she turned, the room was swimming with children.

In late October, Roddy was lying on the table in the finch room. His eyes were open, and he was looking at a half-opened window in the skylight. A bird flew across it. He heard the door open, but didn't look up. Steps went past him, and through the cages he could see the back of Mary Leibnitz's head. He heard her walk to where José Jacinto Flores kept his lovebirds and tropical fish. Through the cheeping of the birds he could hear Spanish being spoken. He heard a chair scrape, then footsteps. Mary walked into the finch room, and Roddy sat up on the table. He looked at her through an opening in the cages, and she stared back like a startled animal. He could not imagine what she was reading on his face, but when he focused he could see what was on hers. It was pure grief; if he had ever seen it before, he hadn't known what it was. He swung his legs around.

"Please don't get up," she said, in a soft voice, and he watched her as she walked slowly past the cages and out the door.

 # the elite viewer

Benno moran sat down to his evening round of television. He thought of this ritual as circular, beginning and ending at the same point—the first and last word of news, or the first and last chirp of the margarine commercial. Now that Charlotte was gone, Benno discovered that he was making some changes in his life. He had not been looking for them especially; he had not expected Charlotte to go away, but she had gotten a fellowship to go to England as part of a two month seminar. The first few days she was gone, the house had seemed strange and uninhabited. Benno felt like a clam reentering its shell. Suddenly he realized what it meant, Charlotte's going away. Once he had been a raw clam in its natural state, a clam with a roommate. Now he was cooked and he decided vaguely, without knowing quite what to do, that it was time to smother himself in butter, or at least to dip his feet in the cocktail sauce.

The first thing Benno thought of was to find some willing, random girl and go to bed with her. But, he reflected, any man can do that, and most men in his present position do. Benno was an industrial inventor. He had recently invented a plastic cartridge that could be inserted into chemical freight cars. Surely he could do better with his wife away than to find some fast girl.

At first it rattled him that he was thinking of things to do—

exotic things to do—because Charlotte was away. After all, he loved Charlotte and he thought that what he was feeling was childish rebellion. It didn't quite make sense. But still, it was the first time in nine years that he had been alone.

He had found the television set by accident, simply turned it on and watched. Several weeks later he realized that watching television was the exotic thing he was doing in Charlotte's absence.

He considered this. When Charlotte was home, they never watched television, not even the news. They had been given a set for a wedding present and it had been turned on four or five times: for inaugurals and assassinations. Charlotte, who taught British history, did not approve of the television set, of newscasters and especially of late-night talk programs. Benno had begun to think of the late-night talk program as some truly corrupting pageant so fanatic was Charlotte's moral outrage at the idea of it. "It's ruining the art of conversation," she said. "Talk about communication gaps. Really, I think my students would listen better if I sang a commercial every half hour or so."

Talk shows were only one of the things Charlotte hated. She hated frozen vegetables and spoke about it. She hated prepackaged cheese that had paper between the slices, and American gin, plastic dishes; she hated orange flavoring, instant iced tea, spaghetti sauce in cans, Corfam, spray bottles, and paperback editions. Furthermore, she refused to wear makeup of any sort or to have her hair styled, and at one time she had threatened to become a vegetarian, but Benno had lured her to her senses with Irish bacon. It was a good thing, Benno often thought, that Charlotte was good-looking, because left to her own devices, she might have been deeply unattractive and never noticed. She was a large, tall woman, with the coloring of a milkmaid, the laugh of a longshoreman, and the legs of a diver. Her hair was straight and as coarse as a horse's mane and it was dark around her white face. She looked at various moments like a Kabuki dancer, a pale Apache warrior, a colt, or Michelangelo's *David,* had it been female. It was all right for her to be natural about herself, Benno thought, because she was so striking, but she wasn't a very good cook, or rather she was a plain cook. In her naturalism she made everything she cooked taste as if it had been boiled with apples and vitamin pills.

He mulled Charlotte over. He was not actively glad she was gone, but he could not have been in his current state of mind if she were here. He was glad she had all her quirks; those were the things he had loved her for first, but they had lived with him for nine years like lice or germs; they had slept with him; they had been intimate with him; they were part of him. He yawned.

Four weeks had passed since Charlotte's departure. The house was as neat as she had left it, but Benno's habits had begun to change. The first week she was gone he had bought a frozen cake, a frozen three-layer cake. He took it out of its icy little box as if it were an icon. It had the consistency of a sponge and tasted like slightly rubbery chocolate. Its frosting was a kind of cherry-flavored whipped gum. He had never seen anything like it. At the first bite, he reeled back with astonishment: it was sublime. The next week he bought several frozen cakes and some candy bars made chiefly of preservatives and artificial coloring. He tried a frozen Mexican dinner, but whatever was sleeping in those little tin trays tasted like hot spiced mud and looked like primal slime. He discovered frozen orange juice, AM radio, ladies' magazines, electric toothbrushes, and thrillers. But it was the discovery of television he loved best of all. He sat before it, beginning with the early evening news, a glass of milk and a slab of frozen cake on a plate, and watched. Often he would turn the sound off and make up lines for the newsmen. He became all the voices on the ads: the hysterical mother anxious about household odor, the bumbling father banished to the garage, the teenage bride with detergent worries. It kept him vastly amused for several weeks, and then he began to get somewhat depressed.

Once at his office, he was useless for an hour every morning, his eyes wincing at the memory of a dark room, sharp gray glare, and dazzling white shirts. He would stare out the window and lean over his drawing board. These days it took quite a while to wake up. When Charlotte was around, he woke up as fast and clean as a freshly snapped twig. Now he crawled out of sleep, like a wounded fly climbing out of a sticky cup. For that hour at work when he was not quite awake, he was the emotional equivalent of a hyperfertile field: everything took instant bloom. Stories in the newspapers touched him. Secretly in the men's room, he wept about the war, the lost and found columns, the return of the wounded soldiers, the brides on the society page. Gradually he became fond of that hour, and savored it like ambrosia.

It was high summer and the streets shimmered out waves of heat that fluttered like lingerie. Dry, parched leaves shriveled on the trees. The office was as cold as a meat locker, and Benno, braised by the pavement, roasted in the subway, and boiled in the elevator, stood in his office basking in the exquisite cool relief. On very hot mornings, he felt as if he were being remorphized into a human as the air-conditioner gradually evaporated his hot, tortured animal sweat. He felt very well, but he was lonesome.

The girl who brought him his coffee every morning was a fat, high-waisted married girl called Sylvia. She interested him only insofar as that her breasts appeared to be perfectly conical. At the moment she was on vacation with her husband, whom Benno imagined to have dents in either side of his chest gouged by his wife's sharp bosom. The girl who brought him his coffee this morning was therefore not Sylvia. Whatever her name was, she was tall and thin with a wide mouth and a row of squat, even teeth. Her hair was an unnatural red and she was wearing a slick little dress made from a plastic fiber that looked slightly musty and wet. On her feet were thin shoes the color of mirrors. "What's your name?" asked Benno, not knowing on which word to put the emphasis.

"Greenie," said the girl, setting the cup on the drawing board.

"Greenie?" asked Benno.

"Yeah," said the girl, looking around the office. It had a drawing board, a wooden work table, and walls of cork for sticking up designs and plans.

"What kind of a name is Greenie?" asked Benno. "Is it really Greenie?"

"Yeah," said the girl. "I swear to God. I don't know what kind of name it is. It's my name. It isn't short for anything." Then she vanished after looking Benno in the eyes for several seconds.

Benno considered her. On the one hand, she was very ugly. On the other hand, she was very beautiful. She had those squat teeth, and squat hands that didn't seem to belong to her tall, thin body. Her technicolor hair was tied back with a brilliant green-and-yellow ribbon. She was flat-chested and had the kind of sparse, bony body that looks as if it will make up in childish, game animation what it lacks in fullness. She seemed a rather simple girl. He thought of the look she had given him, and he remembered that she had very queer eyes. They were a fairly run-of-the-mill amberish brown, but whereas most people's eyes turned color, or changed expression, her eyes shifted from one extreme to the other while the rest of her face remained perfectly frozen except for her jaw, which lifted itself only to chew gum. Her eyes had been, from second to second, intelligent and piercing and then completely blank and vacant. What a nice girl, he thought, Greenie. She had a fairly lowish voice that was tarred by her adenoids and feathered by her cigarettes, which made it slightly husky. It was pretty effective.

Greenie was incandescent. She wore silvery powder, pearlized makeup, and vaseline on her eyebrows. She went off like a flashbulb. On the hot subways, crowds turned rank, rotted, and brown like jungle vegetation, but Greenie—he imagined her—Greenie would stand unaffected, her face a perfect, unmoving waxy mask of that silver stuff she shone with. Benno closed his door and sipped his coffee.

At lunchtime, Greenie reappeared. In her nasal voice she said, "Want lunch?"

Without thinking he said: "If you do."

And she said: "You can buy it for me."

He said: "If you eat it with me." And she nodded. Benno thought this was one of the most romantic conversations he had ever had.

For lunch, Greenie had cherry soda, shrimp salad on pale white bread, potato chips, a chocolate drink, and a Mars bar. Benno had roast beef on dry toast. He sat drinking his coffee with his feet up. Greenie sat in a wicker chair with her legs twined around each other. Benno felt a surge of love, admiration, and cheer. She was awfully nice and very easy in a way that suggested she was either insane, or perfectly level.

"What's your last name, Greenie?" Benno asked.

"Frenzel," said Greenie. Up close, freckles appeared under her silvery powder. Her hair was like a coiled piece of copper and smelled of perfume and lacquer. She took off her shoes and put her feet up. Benno noticed that she had painted her toenails pearly pink. He was stupefied, astonished and filled with happiness. She was a walking museum of wonders, Benno thought.

"What do you do here, Greenie?" Benno asked.

"I'm taking over for Sylvia. You think she's on vacation, and she is, but she isn't coming back. She's gonna have a baby." Greenie handed him a chocolate cupcake, filled with cream. "She told me to have a look at you."

"Oh?" said Benno.

"Yeah," said Greenie, smoking. "She said you were pretty nice."

"Am I?" asked Benno, in a tone of unsure passion.

"Yeah," said Greenie in her post nasal drip voice. "Shaw." She enunciated certainty as if announcing the name of the playwright. She gathered up the cups and napkins and wrappings, and disappeared.

For two weeks, Greenie was his lunch companion. At night, Benno peopled his television ads with her, substituting her face for those of the actresses, and, watching the news, he heard the events of the day recited through her husky, adenoidal voice. All the girls dancing for cleaner laundry were attached to her legs. At night, he dreamed bright dreams in which fruit dropped out of trees and burst in Technicolor at his feet. Girls floated on green lawns, and Greenie did an ad in television black and white for cat food. In his dream, Greenie was a cat. She was complete cat, complete woman. She was lying down wearing a dress. Her eyes had a slightly amused look, a look of hers he had recently discovered and she cooed out of a round mouth: "Every cat is a woman. Every woman is a cat." In her hand she held a can of tuna fish.

In the mornings, now, there was a knife edge on his bleariness. Every hair on his body, every cilia sensitized itself to pick up Greenie. He could feel the television-broken veins in his eyes strain to see every possible bit of her. She brought the coffee and before lunch said very little except, "Yeah, shaw."

After several lunches, Benno found out that she was twenty-three, that she had a boyfriend called Roger whom she "liked fine," that she had quit college after two years, and that she wore a size nine narrow shoe. She lived with her sister in Brooklyn; her parents had retired and moved to California. Benno gathered they were rather agèd. Her sister, she explained, was a beatnik who had married a stockbroker, and they had a house in Brooklyn Heights, or at least the stockbroker did, and everybody thought that she, Greenie, was very rich when actually, she said in a flat monotone, her brother-in-law was rich but she had to pay room and board.

At lunch, Greenie put her feet up and ate Oreo cookies and smoked. She drank cherry soda and had tuna fish with extra mayo every day except Friday, when she had shrimp salad. She answered his questions at length and said, "Yeah, shaw." The air-conditioner hummed tunelessly.

One afternoon, they got up at the same time to get the coffee, and Benno caught the image of the two of them in the mirror.

He was tall and solid and looked like anything dark: Portuguese, Armenian, Lebanese, Puerto Rican. Benno had a wide face with a flat nose, and eyes that were very dark in color, but almost transparent, like cooked sugar. Actually he was a nice Jewish boy whose mother was Russian. He was tall and woodsy, and his hair was very thick and cut so that it looked very long when it was actually quite short. Greenie, next to him, was an apparition. She wore an electric blue dress made of artificial silk with five enamel rings on her right hand. She wore blue plastic shoes and her hair was done in burnished curls around her silvery face.

On Friday, Benno said, "Will you have dinner with me?"

"Yeah," said Greenie.

"At my house?"

"You married guys kill me," Greenie said without inflection.

"My wife is away," said Benno.

"Yeah," said Greenie, rubbing her lower lip. "Yeah." She sat down and then got up. "Yeah, shaw," she said.

Through the afternoon, she assumed a phlegmatic silence and walked rather heavily, clattering her heels. At three o'clock, she brought him his afternoon coffee. She sat in his chair and smoked. The cigarettes she smoked were mentholated and smelled like the air-conditioned inside of a cheap drugstore, and the stubs she left in the ashtray had a rim of pearly pink around the filter.

Out on the street, they walked stiffly. It was more than hot: it was like being under a damp blanket in the tropics. The sky was heavy and yellow, the air hung in layers too wet to rise, and the headline of the evening paper indicated that the air pollution index was unhealthy. Benno's collar melted and his suit turned to Pablum. Greenie, next to him, lived in an air-conditioned world of her own that followed her wherever she went. Not a ringlet drooped. His face, washed with sweat and soot, felt gray, but she was the pearl of the Orient, and where the soot fell freely on the populace, it had enough sense to stay away from her.

Charlotte had chosen their apartment because it was plain, because it was spacious, and because it had good light. Since she needed absolute darkness to get to sleep, blackout shades had been provided for all the windows (including the living room in case she should want to nap on the couch). Benno kept the shades down, and the apartment when they entered it was dark and cold. It was like walking into a cave. They stood in the hall recovering and then Benno took Greenie into the den and offered her the leather chair. He sat on a burlap sofa and they drank cherry soda, which he had bought on the way home.

" 'S nice room," said Greenie. Benno looked around. It was a nice room—a nice, plain, bare room and she looked like the Albert Memorial in it. He was very glad she was there.

"It's six o'clock," he said. "Do you want to watch the news?"

"Yeah," said Greenie. "Shaw. I always watch the news." He turned on the set. It glowed like a fungus. "What's on tonight?" asked Greenie.

"I don't know," said Benno. "I just turn the dial and find out."

"Well, that's dumb," Greenie said. "That way you could be missing something good. Gimme the paper." She went carefully down the listings and with a red pencil worked circles around the night's program. "See?" she said. "That's all the good stuff."

They watched the news and Benno turned the sound off and did his imitations. "That's pretty funny," she said. "You don't look like the type to horse around like that."

"What about dinner?" Benno asked.

" 'S too hot. You gimme some money and I'll go down to the deli and get some stuff and we can watch T.V."

She came back from the delicatessen with a shopping bag. Her hair had unraveled slightly and hung in her face. Benno realized that he thought she was the most beautiful girl he had ever seen.

"Look," she announced nasally. "I got cheese, ham, mustard, cherry soda, beer, and some cupcakes." In addition to which she had bought a package of lemon Kool-Aid, two readymade tuna fish sandwiches, a large jar of mayonnaise, a frozen cake, and some plastic spoons. "It'll be like a picnic," Greenie said, and made sandwiches on the rug. They drank cherry soda out of the bottle while they watched a program called "Mr. Wilson's Dream Wife," which Benno insisted on. Mr. Wilson's real wife was an outrageous shrew, but Mr. Wilson had found that if he simply turned a dial on the machine he had bought for forty-five cents in a junk store, Mrs. Wilson turned into a sleek, blonde sylph who said only yes, or no, breathily.

"You only like this show 'cuz your wife is away," said Greenie.

"That isn't so," said Benno. "My wife is very beautiful and she's not at all like Mrs. Wilson. I watch it because it's a *good* show."

"Yeah," said Greenie, nibbling her way through her second tuna fish sandwich. "Shaw."

They watched "Horror Theater" sitting on the couch, and when it became particularly horrible, they clung together. During "World of Romance," Benno kissed Greenie. On the screen, Laura was kissing Jim just before he went to find the gang that had wounded his brother. Kissing Greenie was a series of diminutive experiences. Her pearlized mouth was slippery with lipstick and tasted of metallic peaches. Her squat teeth pressed against his lips. She tasted like minty smoke, cherry syrup, chocolate cupcake.

As "World of Romance" flickered off, two animated sticks of margarine executed a two step.

"Listen, Greenie. The Moscow Philharmonic is on the educational station. Would you mind?"

"Naa," said Greenie, who smiled when the screen crowded up with unkempt men in evening dress. She sat like a bored but polite child. During a crescendo, Greenie grabbed him, knocked him off balance, and kissed him.

"What's it gonna be," said Greenie.

"What do you mean?" asked Benno, who understood. "What about Roger?"

"I'm mad at Roger. He can go to hell."

"But, I mean, Greenie, this is pretty serious stuff. I mean, we work together every day, and all. It would be very difficult."

Greenie lifted an eyebrow. "How old are you?" she asked.

"Thirty-six," said Benno.

"You must be outa your mind," she said. "Talk about the generation gap."

"What do you mean, Greenie?"

"Oh, come off it. I'm mad at my boyfriend, and your wife is away and you think it's all life and death."

"But it's serious, Greenie."

'Yeah, shaw," she smirked.

"How isn't it serious, then?"

"If you don't know, baby, I can't tell you. It just isn't, but it is now 'cuz you're making an issue of it."

"O.K., Greenie," said Benno, grabbing her around the wrist. "Let's go."

"Go where?"

"To the bedroom."

"Bedroom?" Greenie shrieked. "Bedroom?" She was laughing. "That's the tackiest thing I ever heard."

"What does that mean, Greenie?"

"Lissen," said Greenie. "You know what Sylvia said about you? She said you were very square. I think it's really kind of cute."

Benno sat and watched her. In her slick little dress she was prancing up and down the room.

"I don't understand what to do with you, Greenie. I don't think you like me," said Benno. His eyes were beginning to hurt from the glare.

"Shaw I like you. I like you fine," said Greenie. She sat down between him and the television set, and changed the channel. "Here's something you'll like," she said, smiling. It was a documentary on nutrition and mental health. For several minutes they watched it sitting perfectly still.

"O.K., come on," said Greenie.

"Come on where?" asked Benno. He had begun to falter. He felt that perhaps he had gone too far.

"Come on and sit on the rug with me," she husked.

"O.K.," said Benno. He sat on the rug with his arm around her bony shoulders. On the screen, a lady psychiatrist was talking about protein levels. With a pearly hand, Greenie changed the channel, again.

"Hello," purred the voice on the set. 'I'm Nancy, your media lady."

"This is fine," said Greenie. "I always like to make love to Nancy the media lady."

"Greenie," said Benno. "Are you certain you know what you're doing?"

"Oh, shaw," she answered. "Nancy the media lady's great."

"I mean . . ." began Benno. He wasn't sure what he meant, or meant to say. In four weeks Charlotte would come home. He felt invaded.

"Greenie . . . do you know what you're doing?"

Greenie grabbed him by the arm and pulled him next to her. "Yeah," she said. "Shaw."

 # dangerous french
mistress

I T IS SAID by some that I am beginning to take on
the mannerisms of an agèd professor, but my friends know that
the life I live is orderly, sober, and not at all cheerless. My suits
are made for me by an old Viennese tailor in Washington Heights.
The material, gray or black or blue, is supplied by a firm of hab-
erdashers in Paris from whom I order direct. After Princeton, I
went to Heidelberg and the Sorbonne, and I am now twenty-nine,
in New York.

The apartment I live in was left to me by a professor of classics
at Barnard, a spinster with no family, a friend of Alden Marshall,
the professor with whom I work. We used to have tea together on
Sunday afternoons, and once she told me that she thought of me as
a son. After she died, I wondered why she accepted me in this
way; after all, she had spent her life unmarried, teaching at a girls'
school.

The apartment has seven large rooms and three smaller ones
off the pantry. It looks over the Hudson and was, when I took
possession, filled with her clothes and books and furniture. The
clothes I gave to the Salvation Army, and the books I didn't want
to the Barnard Library. All the Greek pots, statues, and ornaments she left to me. They are dusted every week by the maid
who has been warned about their extreme fragility. The furniture,

also left to me, was either good Shaker replica, Colonial American (clearly heirlooms from her family), or French provincial, all of which I kept.

I wondered why she had maintained so large an apartment, but as Alden Marshall says, events collide in this world, so perhaps I collided with the apartment she was saving 'and her need for a son. But the apartment was too large for me, and, finally, too expensive. I had cut down my teaching to two classes a week so I would have more time for my thesis and book. My name was on the lease, and I decided I would find someone to share the rent. When I got married, whoever it was would leave and the apartment would be mine for my family.

Opportunities overlap in life, and six months after I moved in, Alden sent me an Egyptian called Anwar P. Soole (the P. I later discovered was for Pasteur: his father was a doctor). Alden had met him in Paris: Anwar was living there but when his visa ran out, he came to New York and looked Alden up. He needed a place to live, so Alden sent him around to me.

Anwar Soole was tall and lean. He reminded me of a greyhound because his spareness tended to diminish his height. He looked shorter than he actually was. His eyes were gray and his skin was the color of smoke. Straight dust-colored hair fell into his eyes. Women find him beautiful or boyish, or both, they tell me. I made him a cup of tea and we discussed not so much the possibility of his moving in, but how to get his five trunks and ten crates from Pier 84 to Riverside Drive. He talked earnestly about his painting and poetry, his eyes rather plaintive and appealing. He sat, literally, on the edge of his chair and the intensity of his expressions was almost stagy. He moved, the way precocious children do, from the serious to the flirtatious and struck an irresistible balance in between. I have since learned that he does this with everyone; he would flirt with inanimate objects if he thought he could get a reaction out of them.

Three days later, Anwar, accompanied by four movers, ten crates, and five trunks, moved in. In a week, he was unpacked and settled. Among his possessions were four Victorian birdcages complete with stuffed birds from Ceylon and India, a collection of jade ornaments that filled four glass cases, another four cases of ancient Egyptian artifacts, eighteen albums of photographs, a small Matisse, fifty or more of his own paintings, a teak bedstead from Pakistan, two tiger skins, several bolts of Egyptian batik, a series of African musical instruments packed in excelsior, a set of old spode, two fourteen-by-twenty Persian rugs, and two hundred books. One crate was filled with huge hunks of polished driftwood from Africa and Egypt that we suspended from wires flush with the wall in the living room. There was also some assorted French porcelain, linen, paint boxes, easels, a typewriter, a clothes press, fourteen suits, twelve jackets, two tuxedos, and a set of copper skillets.

My own things, some glass portraits of my ancestors, some painted trunks from my Pennsylvania Dutch ancestors, the paintings and photographs I acquired in Paris and Heidelberg, and the dishes Hattie Marshall had given me, lived comfortably with Anwar's litter. The tiger skins stretched gracefully on the wooden floor of the living room.

Alden Marshall had taught me aesthetics at Princeton. He was seventy-five and Hattie, his wife, was seventy-three. They lived two buildings down from me on Riverside Drive. We were working together on what he said was his last book and our drafts were typed by his occasional secretary, a pale, plain, regular-featured girl named Lilly Gillette. Alden and Hattie, old and slightly preoccupied, scarcely noticed her. She appeared at the doorway and stacked the clean typed sheets on the desk, silent as a ghost. She seemed to require no notice at all, so it was unexpected—it was shocking—when she appeared at my door one afternoon. I had no idea what she wanted: Alden hadn't sent her, she had no drafts or pages for me to correct. After a conversation about which I can remember nothing, she seduced me and left.

She was middle-sized and blonde, and could have been anywhere between twenty and thirty. Her face showed nothing: she was vacant, but not passive. One of her eyes was green, and one was blue. This disparity gave her the facial profundity that statues with no eyes at all have. Looking at her, I remembered a white barn cat I once saw that had a blue eye and a green eye. It had the same sort of depth to its look that Lilly had to hers, but it was only one of nature's tricks. It was impossible to tell if Lilly had any more depth to her than the cat. Her presence was almost neutral, her clothes were neutral. They fitted her like an extra skin, which is not to say that they were tight, but she wore them like a skin she lived in and paid no attention to. It was impossible to remember what she wore. Sitting in a chair, the chair diminished her; you noticed a chair containing a girl, not a girl sitting in a chair.

She stood at the door to my apartment.

"Phillip Hartman," she said.

"Yes," I said. "You're Alden's secretary."

"Right."

I gave her a questioning look, but since she said nothing and was carrying nothing, and since her look revealed nothing, I walked into my study, making way for her to follow.

She sat in the chair by my desk smoking a cigarette while I smoked a cigar. She looked over the rows of books, the glass pictures, the photographs, the large French vases. She looked to the bed, partially obscured by a bookshelf at the far end of the room. It seemed to place her: when she found it—I was following her eyes—she stopped looking. We must have had some conversation, but as I said, I cannot remember what about. I went to the kitchen to make a pot of tea and when I brought it back on a tray, with cups and milk, I found her standing by the bed. She had turned back the covers. Her clothes were on the floor.

We became lovers, if that term is appropriate, and she left without a word, leaving not a hair on the pillow, or cigarette stub (she had emptied the ashtray while I made the tea), not one smudge of herself. We did not have dinner, she did not offer to cook or ask to be taken out. She put on her clothes and left.

"Don't get up," was all she said. The tea, untouched, was cold in its pot.

It was an event so unadorned that it took me a week to realize that I was catching my breath. After she left, I spent several hours looking for a book I thought was on my desk, but it was on a shelf where it should not have been. I have my books by subject —one shelf is art history, one philosophy, and one literature. They are alphabetized by author on each shelf. I was looking for a volume of Winkelmann and found it wedged beside a copy of *Ulysses,* upside down.

On Tuesdays I have lunch with Alden Marshall at the Faculty Club. On Thursdays I have dinner with him and Hattie at their apartment or we go to a restaurant. Tuesdays and Thursdays we work on his book, Mondays and Fridays I teach. The rest of the time is for my thesis and my own work.

Lilly Gillette sat in Alden Marshall's study opening his letters with an ivory knife. Her face was impassive as a board and did not change when I came in.

Alden and I spent the morning working. Lilly brought him his mail and some typed pages. When I got back from lunch, she was at my door. I felt a lurch go through me, as if my bones quaked. She followed me down the hall to my study. This time we had no conversation at all. I looked down into her face for anger, or love or tenderness or confusion, but found only bland acceptance. Her departure then was a replica of the first. She said, "Don't get up," and left.

          Anwar Soole was out more than he was in, but we frequently collided. He called me "Filipo" and made me help him hang his paintings. Once in a while he would cook a huge Middle Eastern meal to which he would invite several of the more luscious students from the girls' college at which he taught, or some elderly specimens of Italian nobility. He had two kinds of friends: dull but opulent girls and Europeans in New York on business. After he had been teaching for several months, the girls turned up, elegant in silk, rustling like expensive leaves and leaving the apartment faintly scented with their perfume. If I was home, they were brought into my study to admire my French vases and glass paintings. Then Anwar made a pot of sweet, acrid coffee that we drank in the living room and watched Anwar drape himself languidly over the tiger skin.

With his girls he was hyperanimated, lithe, and springy. He did parodies, imitations, little dances. He acted out hour-long comedies, taking all the parts. At parties he danced wildly, almost ridiculously I thought, until one of his more intelligent consorts said, "He looks silly, but he's actually graceful. He has the best balance I've ever seen." She was right, of course: Anwar could stand on one foot for ten minutes and almost twist his other leg around his waist.

Once in a while he would turn up at the apartment with a really magnificent girl. The more beautiful they were, the less English they spoke. One of these was an extremely tall, catlike German and I was produced to help him out. Anwar spoke Italian, French, Arabic, and English, but no German, so he was helpless. Since you cannot translate manic charm, the evening was a waste for him, and the girl, who was quite nice and fairly intelligent, was leaving for Munich the next day.

After a ferocious night at a party, blasting out all his energy, he would spend the next day painting in the studio he had created of the pantry rooms, getting it back. Several times during the winter, after weeks of frantic activity, he would get sick, so sick that I had to bring his food to him on a tray. Sick, he looked tiny, dark gray against the white sheets, and when he slept his features assumed the meek austerity of a child's. Without his energy he was puzzled, frightened, and torpid. After a week ailing, he was up. The girls were in, or he was out. After a week of being out, he was domestically in, badgering Minnie, the maid who came in twice a week, or cooking his elaborate meals, or rearranging his studio. Since we both had social obligations to repay, we had a formal party during which Anwar drank from the silver punch bowl, danced nonstop for three hours, threatened to throw a dish of salad at the girl who had told me how perfect his balance was, and stood on his head. This went mostly unnoticed because there were about seventy people there. He was like a man racing on a tightrope, stumbling but never falling. The rhythm of his life was energy, dissipation, sickness, and recuperation. When his ancient Europeans came to dinner, he was grotesquely correct.

There was no pattern to Lilly's visitations. I am not a bad-looking man but I am hardly the sort of person women crazed with lust pursue. Nothing like Lilly had ever happened to me, and the women I had known, several of whom I loved—a girl I had lived with in Heidelberg, an American girl in Paris I had wanted to marry, were rather like me; mild, scholarly, cerebral. "Intellectual sensualists" is the term the girl in Paris invented for people like us. But here was Lilly Gillette, stolid, silent, bland, standing at my doorway, Monday afternoon, Thursday at two in the morning, Friday at lunchtime after my class. She never spent the night. She never drank so much as a glass of water. We barely talked at all and it was my fault, I often think, because I was so baffled, so buffaloed, and although I did not allow myself to know it, so disturbed that I simply *couldn't* speak. How was I to start a conversation with a woman I had been to bed with fifteen, twenty times? Lying next to her, in the few minutes she gave herself for lying next to me, sentences blurted their way to the beginning of speech: elephantine sentences, all of which began with why. Why are you here? Why did you start this? Why me? Her whole presence said: there is nothing to say—so how could I ask? Sometimes a week would pass and I would see her only at Alden's. No Lilly at my door. Those nights I would lie half asleep, the possibility of full sleep disturbed, waiting for the doorbell to ring. A key would turn and I could hear Anwar's feet, sometimes two sets of footsteps, go quietly down the hall to his room, hear muffled laughter. Those nights I wondered how to start a conversation about something that had been going on for months. Each time she saw me, she said my name, Phillip Hartman, identifying me in the way one might classify a moth or bug. She never called me by name, except when she saw me; but then, how could she? We never spoke.

Twice a week, Minnie Hoskins came to clean. If Anwar was around, she got almost nothing done. He turned up the portable radio Minnie carried with her everywhere she went and danced with her. She was a large, pecan-colored grandmother. If I came home and Anwar had been in, there would be Minnie, holding her broom, giggling.

"That Anwar. He do make me laugh," Minnie said.

"Minnie," I said to her one day, about four months after Lilly's first visitation, "when you dust my books, be sure to put them back in order. They're all out of place now. I can't find anything I'm looking for."

"I vacuum your books. I never take nothing off the shelf," said Minnie.

"Well, it's very perplexing," I said. "None of them are where they're supposed to be."

"You ask that Anwar," Minnie said. "Maybe he been foolin' in your room."

I asked him.

"Filipo," he said. "You have nothing in your room I would ever want to read."

"But the books are all out of order," I said.

"Perhaps you are in the middle of a nervous breakdown and know not what you do," Anwar said. "Everyone in New York has a nervous breakdown. You could be having one yourself."

At four o'clock in the morning, the doorbell rang. It was one of Anwar's nights out, so it could have been Anwar. But it was Lilly, smoking a cigarette. She was wearing a raincoat, a shirt, and a pair of jeans.

"I don't understand you," I said. "I don't understand what you want."

"I don't want anything. I just came over."

"At four in the morning?"

"The pipes burst in my building," she said. "I don't have any water."

It was the first time she ever spent the night. The next morning I made her a cup of coffee and brought it to her. She held it for a moment, and then put it on the night table. She watched me as I got dressed, immobile and disinterested.

"I'm leaving," I said. She nodded her head slightly in acknowledgment.

When I got home the bed was made. The cup on the night table was full of cold, untouched coffee. The milk in it had curdled and shredded on the surface. The books were out of order.

Lilly was listed in the telephone directory. I had never called her, never, in fact, had known where she lived.

She picked the phone up on the fourth ring.

"Do you put my books out of order?" I said.

"Yes."

"Why?"

"I look at them and forget where I got them from."

"I see," I said.

"Goodbye," Lilly said.

I put the telephone down, invaded by a kind of despair. People are abandoned by their lovers, their spouses, their parents—and despair, lose their jobs or loved ones, and grieve. What had abandoned me was explanation. Perhaps it is a disease scholars suffer when reason deserts. It seemed to me I had been incorporated into an event for which there was no explanation, a vacuum that sucked in misery.

If I had been held up or robbed, I felt I would have understood a progression of circumstances: someone was hungry or withdrawing from heroin and I passed by and was therefore mugged. But I felt I had been vandalized maliciously, gratuitously. Although my books stood gleaming on their shelves, none of them missing, they were out of order.

On his petulant days, Anwar referred to me as Fra Filipo, and called my room "the cell." He claimed I lived like a monk, although I had told him about Jane Pinkham, the American girl in Paris, whom I wanted to marry and who was coming back to New York. I wondered what Anwar would say if he knew that sometimes nightly, sometimes weekly, in the mornings or afternoons, a girl appeared who seemed to have no further interest in me beyond a couple of hours in bed. I carried this fact around in a little sling of smugness.

Two days after the telephone call, I came home from a morning of work with Alden to find Lilly in my bed, staring at the ceiling.

"How did you get in?"

"Your roommate let me in," she said.

A sense of spoilage came over me, as if someone had sprung my plans for a surprise party or had taken the trump card from my hand and revealed it to me, smiling.

"I don't understand you," I said. "Why do you keep coming here?"

"If you don't want me around," Lilly said, "just say."

"Would it stop you if I did?"

"I don't know what would stop me from anything," said Lilly Gillette. In novels, in movies, in plays, the hero looks deeply into the eyes of his girl and the audience sees that they have blundered into an understanding that changes things between them. I looked into the eyes of my girl, but she wasn't my girl, and she did not look back. This was no novel or movie—it didn't even seem to be life—and there was no audience. She looked at the ceiling, her head tilted toward her left shoulder. Some unsettled feeling caught me, some point where rage and tenderness fused. I wanted either to strike or comfort her, but, so paralyzed by a situation of forced silence, I did neither.

Anwar, over coffee, read from *France-Soir*. "The victim," he translated. "A Swede in the coffee business in France for two months said that his car was wrecked by a girl with whom he had a casual liaison. He described her as a dangerous French mistress type. When pressed for explanation, M. Bølstrom would say only that she was an extremely emotional and volatile person and had taken his car after an argument. The woman, whose identity has not been made public, is a French Canadian student, M. Bølstrom said."

"That's what you need, Filipo," he said, "a nice dangerous French mistress type, cut from the pages of *France-Soir*."

I looked at Anwar, whose face was feline and puckish. He lapsed into an imitation of the Swedish coffee man and his interviewer from the newspaper, until he got the laugh he wanted out of me. As he washed the dishes he said, "Cheer up, Filipo. You don't even have a car."

The days went by. At night I slept with the windows open, struggling into sleep, waking out of dreams. It seemed that any sound sleep I got was pierced by the doorbell: Lilly, the ends of her pale hair wet with rain, or soft and cottony with mist. If this had been happening to someone else, and had been told to me as a story, if this thing with Lilly had been described to me, if I could *see* it, I would have lit a cigar, smiling as the smoke trailed out the window, and said: "Things like this happen in books and movies, not in life."

My life, which had a comfortable, likable, productive shape to it, had incorporated something—someone—I didn't understand. But it must have fit, because it had happened, and kept happening. One afternoon I asked Lilly if she would like to come to Alden Marshall's party with me. She didn't answer and when I asked again, she said no.

What was there between us? And if I didn't know, how could I ask her? I racked my brain for a starting place, thought of sitting her down to ask what this was all about. Instead, it just went on, erratic visits, one after another. The months that had unraveled between us made the search for a starting place inappropriate, grotesque. If she stayed the night, which she did infrequently, I came home to find my books out of order, and once, one of the French vases turned on its side. There had been flowers in it and some petals lay scattered on the dark spot where water had seeped into the rug.

I had never been to Lilly's apartment. I didn't know how she lived, what she read, what pictures were on her walls. Nothing warm or recognizable operated between us. After what I now realize was a long and anguished time, I thought she was pursuing me, but I was pursuing myself. I put my books back into order, sopped up the wet rug with a cloth, and put the vase upright. There were days when I came home from a morning or afternoon of hard work with Alden, or from the ease of dinner with him and Hattie, expecting to find my apartment ransacked, my vases split and shattered, the glass paintings splintered, the photographs ripped from the wall, my books pulled from the shelves, lying on their broken spines. Boris Godunov says: I cannot sleep, yet I have nightmares. My waking dream was of coming home to this landscape, and in the corner of it was Lilly, smoking in my chair, Lilly the vandal who would say nothing, explain nothing. She would walk over the broken books to the bed and sit upon it, and I, mute uncomprehending walrus, would follow, since I could not find any appropriate place in our silence to ask her what she'd done.

But it never happened. The vase on the rug might have been knocked over by her raincoat as she threw it over her shoulder. The books misplaced and upside down might have been the result of uncaring, blind, vacuity. Still, mornings, afternoons, twilights, dusks, the bell rang, I answered it, it was Lilly and she got, presumably, exactly what she came for.

What I did not know at the time was that on her first visit, it was not me, but Anwar, she was looking for. A few of the nights on which she did not ring the bell, it was her set of footsteps I heard behind his, trailing down the hall. The afternoon I found her lying in *my* bed, she had wakened that morning in Anwar's. He had gone to school and she had simply transferred

herself to me, so she had not lied when she said that he had let
her in.

After this was revealed to me, I wondered if I had never asked
her anything because I would have hated to know. When I did ask
her, it was in Alden's study, not mine. He and Hattie had gone to
Maine for two weeks. I, of course, had a key, and Alden had asked
me to check his mail and water the plants. Lilly obviously had a
key too. When I let myself in, I heard typing from the study and
thought that Alden had delayed his trip. But it was Lilly, as pale
as the paper she was typing on, as bland as bread. I wondered if
she had trained herself not to look up at the sound of someone at
the door.

"I could have been a burglar," I said. "You didn't even look
up."

"Looking up wouldn't make much difference to a burglar," she
said, above the clacking of the typewriter. Watching her, it seemed
to me that she was either totally innocent or totally insane, or had
perfected a style of evasiveness so intense it nullified her. It was
horrible—but I had let it live beside me.

I spun her swivel chair around. Her eyes fixed on my mouth, as
if she were a deaf mute priming to read lips.

"Lilly, listen to me. I don't know what you're after, but I want
to know. You can't live like a specter, appearing at odd hours.
You don't love me, you don't know anything about me and I don't
know anything about you. Would you please tell me what has been
going on."

"If you don't want me to come around, just say," she said.

"I want to know why you came around in the first place."

"I was looking for Anwar," she said. "And he wasn't home."

"Anwar?"

"Your roommate. I didn't know he was your roommate. He
said it was someone called Filipo."

And then she told me that she had spent nights with Anwar
while I slept down the hall, that she had gone from one bed to the
other the afternoon I found her in my room.

"Does Anwar know this?" I said.

"He never asked," Lilly said. "How would he know? You can tell him if you want."

"Don't you care?"

"Not especially," said Lilly.

That was the last contact I had with her. She stopped working for Alden. If I think about it, it is like a dark fairy tale in which the magic word is said and the riches disappear, except there were no riches to disappear. After that conversation, her visits stopped.

Anwar's ladies troop in and out. Alden and I work on his book and I follow my schedule. Thursdays I have dinner with Alden and Hattie. Jane Pinkham, the American girl, is coming to New York from Paris, she writes, and I am to meet her at the airport.

Sometimes a streak of terror goes past me, like a shooting star, close enough to singe my coat. I think: what did Lilly want? Was she only mute, as mute as I was? Did I misunderstand, perform a cruelty? Was she in some state of acute distress, and I unable to help her?

But then I think that spilling my vase and leaving my books where they did not belong were only a short step away from carnage and chaos, and that my waking nightmare was the logical conclusion of what she was up to.

She must still work around here, since I have seen her on the street several times. We salute each other formally, with a diminutive flick of the head.

 # the water rats

IN THE BEGINNING of the spring, geese flew in V
formation. Max watched them from the bay window. He looked
out over the water and saw the first of the small craft battling its
way to an old mooring. On the weekends he liked to sit by the
bay window and watch his part of the Sound. It soothed him, and
it gave him a sense of propriety to see the latticework gazebo, firm
on its slope. A family of barn swallows was building a nest in its
thatched roof. The spot Max watched was ringed by dense firs
where the Sound was squeezed into an inlet. The wind made the
water choppy and there were white tongues on the tops of the
waves.

Recently, Max had discovered that there were water rats in his
part of the Sound. His four children played by the shore and reported that they had seen brown cats swimming there. Max called
the Town Commission and the commission secretary suggested
poison, but in the summer his babies swam face down, splashing
and lapping, and Max asked if there was anything else he could
do.

"I don't know what to tell you, Mr. Waltzer," the secretary said
to Max. "There's a poison that kills only rats and is safe for children and pets, if you want to use it." But Max said he didn't want
poison in his water.

49

That Saturday, Max consulted Eddie Crater, the local vegetable man, who was known to be an occasional hunter. Every Saturday he drove his truck up the Waltzers' driveway—Olivia Waltzer had a standing order for lettuce and tomatoes. Eddie was a large, tall man, about as tall as Max, but he didn't slump as Max often did. Max took him aside and told him about the rats and his reluctance to use poison.

"I think you'll have to shoot them," Eddie said. "I can understand how you feel about poison."

"I don't have anything to shoot them with," said Max. "I haven't fired a gun in years."

"I've got two rifles. I go after ducks sometimes during the season."

"They make a hell of a lot of noise," Max said. "I don't want the kids to be frightened."

"Look," Eddie said. "There was a bunch of wild toms in the woods behind our house, fighting with our cats and tearing them to shreds. I had to shoot them. My wife took the kids to her mother's and that was the last trouble we had with toms. You get the kids out and call me and we'll take care of things. It's probably one nest, but it might be a whole pack. Anyway, you call."

Late one Sunday afternoon, Eddie Crater arrived with his guns. Olivia had taken the children to the city for the day and the house was flat and silent without them. Max had turned on all the lights but it was dim without his family. The air was wet and heavy as Max and Eddie walked down the slope to the water. Max looked back at his house. It was twilight and the upstairs windows were yellow with light. The water was still and the rats made soft, slapping sounds as they swam in circles.

At the first crack, Max was startled. He had forgotten what guns sounded like. It was Eddie's shot and the hit rat was knocked into the air. Then it fell abruptly into the water, trailing blood. They shot four rats in all, and the water was brown and purple with blood. Max and Eddie scooped the bodies up with crab nets and dumped them into a plastic bag. They put the bag into the trash and went into the living room to have a glass of beer.

"You keep an eye out," Eddie said. "I don't know if we got them all. We may have frightened off the rest of them and they could come back."

When Eddie went home, Max paced the length of his large, empty house. Alone, he felt suspended between restlessness and calm. Even when Olivia and the children were there, he thought about them constantly. He felt that they lived in his heart. At times when he was stretched on the sofa reading or gazing at the water, he felt his life was filled with a loveliness so intense he wondered how he contained it. His children spoke and laughed and shouted and sang: they were four boys with dark-blond hair, and he couldn't get over them. When he went to their rooms to kiss them goodnight, he was overwhelmed by the tiny veins in their translucent foreheads. Before he and Olivia went to bed, he stood at the thresholds of their rooms. Then he would go in and kiss them while they slept. They would be slightly damp, smelling of talcum and milk. When he went to his own bedroom, Olivia would be reading. She read the way little girls in old-fashioned novels are drawn reading: the book was open on her lap and she bent down to it.

Max was tall and pale. He walked with his shoulders slightly bent and his head a little bowed as if he were expecting to walk through a low door. He had pale-blond hair and amber-colored eyes set in a wide, mild face. His father had owned an unsuccessful glass bottle factory to which he had been devoted, and when he died Max took over the business. He liked glass: he liked the shape of the chunky green bottles coming off the line. In the fifth year of his ownership, Max had invented a shatterproof glass that was extremely thin, and it had made him rich—rich enough so that six years ago he and Olivia had bought the huge stone house for more money than Max had ever dreamed he would have. It was an old house and had been in the same family for many years. Max had it gutted and stripped, making large, graceful rooms out of the cramped, tight spaces. Huge panes of glass, Max's shatterproof glass, formed the bay windows at the back of the house. Then Max and Olivia and the boys—Hamish, Sandy, Paul, and Scottie—moved in.

Max was still in love with the house. Six years had not dulled his amazement that he owned it. He was in love with his wife and his babies. Looking at his sons, watching their bright heads move as they played, caused him to count his blessings with a sense of pain: he did not understand why all this was his, and he treasured it.

The summer went by placidly. The babies splashed and played in the Sound. Hamish and Sandy built forts around the inlet and staged Indian raids on the lawn. Scottie, the youngest, held tea parties in the gazebo for his imaginary friends. Paul began a collection of birds' eggs that he displayed on sweat socks in the potting shed. Sometimes in the mornings they played on the front lawn with the Tanner boys from down the road. When the babies went swimming that summer, Max or Olivia or both of them went along to watch for rats. After lunch, Paul and Scottie napped and Hamish and Sandy disappeared into the woods. A beautiful quiet filled the house. Olivia played the piano and Max lay on the sofa listening. She played Chopin and Soler. He would lean back against the cushions and let the music mix with the quiet. It seeped into him and he felt it was another gift.

When autumn approached, Max began patrolling for rats. They hadn't reappeared all summer, but Max waited by the water with Eddie Crater's shotgun in his arms. Often he patrolled late at night after Olivia and the babies were asleep. The first frost had come and the grass was brown and trampled. He was warm and sleepy. He was not sure what was driving him out of his bed, into his clothes, and out to the cold Sound. It wasn't restlessness, but he couldn't sleep. He was being compelled. Once he got to the water, he felt a sense of calm. It seemed to him that what he was doing was right. It was part of his life, like getting up in the morning and going to work. He remembered his first days in the house; what a happy fool he had been, splattered with plaster, paint-stained. The workmen had teased him and smiled as they went over the plans. What a halo everything had had around it. He walked several times around the inlet and then back to the house. Inside he savored its sweet smell, the way the walls gleamed as he climbed the stairs. It was worth a walk in the cold to appreciate this. The house seemed to sleep as he walked quietly to the bedroom and got into bed carefully so as not to waken Olivia.

.In December, Max patrolled the water's edge three times a day: before he went to work, when he came home, and once before he went to bed. He knew Olivia was disturbed by this. When he put on his hunting jacket and boots and went to the cupboard for Eddie Crater's shotgun, she watched him with a mixture of puzzlement and concern. But she said nothing and Max knew her silence was a form of trust. He thought of these patrols as brisk, fifteen-minute walks. He found that he liked the night patrol best, when nothing stirred, when the lights from the house expanded on the water, when everything was his. He liked being out when everything was asleep and the water breathed evenly. At times the silence was broken—a dog barking, something snapping in the woods, a dead limb cracking off a tree. Max waited for these punctuations. Sometimes he stood looking at the house which contained everything he loved. He stared at it as if it satisfied a hunger.

As the winter went by, Max's patrols got longer. At night he often stayed out for two hours. There was a flat stone by the water's edge and Max sat there with the gun on his knees. It was a cold, wet winter and the sky was constantly gray and swollen. Finally there was a storm and it snowed for two days. Huge drifts piled up in the front of the house and the back lawn was thick with it. The foam on the Sound froze and ice crusted the sand. Patrolling, Max kicked lumps of icy seaweed with his boot.

In February there was a brief thaw and then an ice storm. Flu broke out in the boys' school and Olivia began to talk about going to Bermuda. She took the children there every year, and Max, if he could get away, came down for a long weekend, but this year he decided that he had too much work. The night before Olivia and the babies left, Max patrolled early. Olivia was sitting on the bed waiting for him when he came in. He took off his boots and his jacket which was stiff with cold.

"I don't want to leave," Olivia said. "I'm worried about you."

"There isn't anything to worry about," said Max. "I'm concerned about all this flu."

Olivia had fine straight hair that was scopped into a coil at the nape of her neck. Her eyes were gray and very steady. She lowered her eyes and asked Max if he were having an affair.

"How can you possibly ask?" said Max. It was like an assault.

"I know you're not," said Olivia. "But I had to ask. I've been desperate about you."

"But nothing's changed between us."

"Max, every morning, every night. For God's sake, it's too cold for dogs to be out, let alone rats. I don't know what's on your mind. I don't understand at all. It upsets me all the time." She began to cry and Max held her in his arms. There was no one in his life except her, and he knew it was something she had to ask. He held her and comforted her, but there was no way for him to explain himself.

"Livvie, Eddie Crater told me I had to be on the lookout. Rats are a serious problem. I don't want them to come back this spring with the kids swimming and all."

"I just don't understand," Olivia said, sobbing. "I understand you all the time, but not this."

"It'll be all right," Max said. "It's all right now. I can't put poison in the water so I have to be sure. Please, Livvie, don't worry. It's a small thing."

The next day he drove them to the airport. It was snowing lightly and flakes flew up against the windshield. The lights craning over the road were fringed with icicles. His children giggled and clowned in the back seat. Max held Olivia's hand and at every stoplight he turned to her and smiled. They waited for the plane in a tight, loving circle, hugging and kissing, until the flight was called. Max watched from the observation deck while the plane took off, and followed it until the clouds covered it.

In the car on the way home, Max was filled with dread. At night mostly, but sometimes during the day, fear assailed him. It was palpable and he could feel it in the area of his heart. It was not disease: he knew that from his yearly checkup. It was terror. Calamities occurred to him, especially alone in the car with his family hovering in the air. He thought of the airplane hanging tenuously in space. He knew life contained profound miseries: something could happen to his children. Hamish was prone to bronchitis, and in his sicknesses Max saw death. Sandy was the most mobile and daring of the four. He was fearless, sprinting from ledges and walls. It only took chance, a hairsbreadth for him to fall and shatter, break his young bones too far from home for help. Paul and Scottie, dreamy infants, could be lured and kidnapped. It happened to other people's children and was reported in the newspapers. He thought of Olivia and the scores of marriages that had smashed around them: if Olivia left him, ceased to love him, got sick. This terrible set of possibilities attacked the shell of his life and put an edge on his happiness. But it seemed to him that life was teaching him the meaning of true happiness, and the secret was that it was difficult and terrifying to be blessed.

It was only chance that he possessed what he had and he had seen what life could do—how it crippled, maimed, killed off, and destroyed. He had seen other people grief-stricken, heartsick, and suffering. Something very different had happened to him. Life had put everything lovely into his hands and had not taken it away. He knew it was not impossible that things would stay this way, but looking at the world, he knew it was improbable. He wondered why the coin of his life didn't turn, show its reverse side and leave him stranded with empty hands. He put on the radio and let the car fill up with music.

When he got home, the total quiet of his house dazed him. He sat on the sofa and added the fear of madness to his catalogue: he was afraid to breathe, afraid to let the thought of his loneliness filter in to him. He realized that if life were to reverse itself and everything he loved was taken away from him, it would resemble this thick, empty silence. He was to live this way for a week, but it seemed unbearable for even fifteen minutes. When Max and Olivia had first met, she remarked that he spent a lot of time staring at her. He knew every plane in her face, every line on her palm, the shape of each of her fingernails. He thought he could enumerate the hairs on his children's bright heads if he were called upon to do so. He stored these things up to have them firmly in his mind should he ever be deprived. After dinner, his family was used to his pushing his chair back and watching them quietly as they finished their coffee and cocoa. If he stared at Olivia, she would say, "Aren't you tired of staring at me after all these years?" And Max would say, "I never get used to anything."

He got up to put on his boots and hunting jacket and took Eddie Crater's rifle out of the locked cupboard. It was dinner time. There was a cold roast in the icebox and a long note taped to the cabinet reminding him where the butter was and when Hattie, the cleaning lady, would be in. He read it and put it in his pocket. It was a love letter from Olivia, who knew he knew the place for every dish, pot, and pan in the kitchen.

He went to the door, about to go out, but the silence of the house drove him back. With the rifle in his hand he went into the dining room, and stood there. He read the grain in the walnut table as if it were print. He memorized how the afternoon light hit the tea service and lit up the back of the curtains. He went from room to room. It was dusk, but he didn't have the heart to turn on any lights. In the living room his eyes went from the rug to the fireplace to the clumsy plaster lumps his children modeled at school, placed on the mantelpiece. He stood in the study, holding in his gunless hand an antique decoy that was as worn and soft as soap. Upstairs he stood at the thresholds of his children's rooms. He went to the bedroom, to the attic, his boots clacking awkwardly against his shins. He realized that he was patrolling his house.

Finally he went out to the Sound and sat on the rock. The earth was spongy beneath his feet and there was thick foam on the sand. A wind came through the pines.

He heard a soft splash in the water and cocked the gun. Something moved in the Sound but in the twilight he couldn't be sure if it was a swell or a rat. He didn't know what to do. The thing surfaced and looked at him. Its eyes glowed like glass. It lifted its sleek head, pulled itself out of the water, and dashed toward the woods. It was a raccoon. Max lifted the gun and aimed at it, but when he realized what he was about to do he walked to the edge of the water, knelt down, and began to cry. Then he got up and hurled the gun out into the Sound as far as he could throw.

When he got back to the house, he took off his wet, cold clothes and sat in his bathrobe in the living room. He was beginning to feel hungry. On his way to the kitchen, the telephone rang. He knew it was Olivia. He picked up the receiver—it was long distance from Bermuda.

"We're all safe," she said. "It's so blue here. The kids are just sitting down to dinner. I miss you."

"I miss you."

"Are you all right? Is everything O.K.?"

"I'm fine," Max said. "Everything is O.K. and I miss you."

"It's only a week," Olivia said. "I love you. Do you have everything you need?"

"Yes," said Max. "Everything."

the girl with the
harlequin glasses

On GUIDO MORRIS'S DESK was a framed photograph that showed Guido and Vincent Cardworthy looking splendid. This photo had been taken on a day when both of them were feeling very cavalier, and reveals them to be tall, lean men in expensive suits. Guido had angled the camera, which had a time exposure, and then rushed behind the desk. Vincent and Guido had been friends since babyhood. In fact, they were second cousins and their states of mind frequently coincided. Their cavalier state manifested itself in large, open smiles, hands thrust forcefully in pockets and heads thrown slightly backward, with appropriate locks of hair falling onto foreheads. On that particular day, Vincent and Guido were filled with an almost anachronistic sense of well-being and optimism. This mood was the occasion for the photo. "If we're feeling this good, we ought to have a record of it," said Guido.

Between them in this photograph, almost obscured by the well-cut shoulders of their jackets, stood Jane Marshall-Howard, the beautiful English girl who at the time had been Guido's surly and inefficient secretary. If there was any hint of tension in the photo, it was in some tiny bunched lines around Guido's eyes: he was brooding about firing Jane. It was going to be difficult, because she was very decorative and because he had grown used to her, in the way one grows used to constant shooting pains. She was always late, she spilled coffee on his papers, and she could only type for five or six minutes until her attention strayed. The day after the picture was taken she told Guido that she had been secretly married to a Brazilian coffee heir and was quitting her job to join her husband, who had recently come into his plantation.

On the afternoon of the day Jane Marshall-Howard quit, Guido's wife called to say that she had gone to stay at her parents' country house for a few months. She felt it would be good for their emotional development. "We should grow separately for a while," she said.

Jane's quitting threw him into the large panic that comes with small change: he did not know what to think about his wife. She told him that she had taken some of her clothes and a few of her books. Barely realizing that he was being committed to living alone among her shoes, bottles, copper pots, and French books, Guido immediately called the employment agency and said that he needed a secretary, and that she must be able to type at least seventy-five words per minute. Then he drank a large glass of seltzer and did nothing more productive for the rest of the afternoon than empty his ashtray.

On the other side of the desk was another photo of Guido and Vincent. This photo was not a record of one of Guido's good moods, but of one of his decisions. Very much obscured, except for a pair of harlequin glasses, was the face of Betty Helen Carnhoops, the girl Guido hired to replace Jane. In this photo, Guido looked faintly pleased because he had hired someone sensible, and Vincent looked aghast but inscrutable. He had just pegged Betty Helen Carnhoops for a truly bad apple.

Vincent said, "How could you hire her after Jane?"

"Jane," muttered Guido, abstractly.

"She's awful," said Vincent.

"She's pleasant. She doesn't take any getting used to." Guido looked absently out of the window. "A pleasant and efficient girl."

Guido and Vincent were both blessed with private incomes, and their sense of work was leisurely. Vincent was a free-lance statistician for the Board of City Planning, and his special field of interest was garbage. He did studies of garbage levels, estimated garbage per dwelling unit, potential garbage crises, and developed theories for the removal of garbage.

Guido had inherited a private foundation called the Magna Carta Trust, which sponsored a literary magazine called *Runnymede,* of which he was the editor.

"How much garbage do you figure Betty Helen Carnhoops and her husband account for?" Guido asked Vincent.

"Who would marry her?" said Vincent.

"She's married to a graduate student in engineering or something," said Guido. "Or chemistry."

"It's the amount of garbage for one squared."

"Isn't it doubled?"

"Squared," growled Vincent. "That girl is a real cup of tainted soup."

"She's perfectly nice," said Guido. "I'm very pleased. She's calm and efficient. The trouble with you is that you've become so jaded that you don't know what agreeable, simple people are like any more."

"The trouble with you, Guido, is that you're very naïve. That girl is a snake."

"She's *my* secretary," Guido said, "and *I* think she's nice."

"But I'm here a lot," said Vincent, mournfully.

Vincent did most of his work in Guido's office. He had a desk in a corner by the window. As a free-lance statistician, he had been given an office by the Board of City Planning, but it was in the shape of an isosceles triangle and it made him feel cramped and slightly dizzy. Guido's office was large and white and airy, with a view of Central Park. Vincent felt he did his best work there. He and Guido spent long afternoons drinking Seltzer and lime juice, watching the sun shine through Guido's collection of glass bowls.

They spent months in indolent, indulgent sloth, followed by a transition into frenzied hard work. Once every quarter Guido produced an issue of *Runnymede,* which was considered magnificent by critics, writers, and subscribers. Once every six months Vincent produced a garbage study that was published in *Urban Affairs Dialogue* and quoted in *The New York Times* and the *City Heretofore.*

Betty Helen Carnhoops was a square girl with piano legs. Her hair was short and efficient. It was of no particular color, although Vincent claimed it was the exact shade of rat fur. She had pale, dampish skin, and her arms were slightly mottled, like Bratwurst. She had pale eyes surrounded by short, spiky lashes. Her harlequin glasses were green plastic and sprouted in each corner a little gold rose with a rhinestone in its center.

"Who would marry her?" said Vincent. He was editing one of his studies entitled: *Technology and the Common Good: New Techniques for Effective Disposal.* "Did you say her husband was a vet?"

"Political science or something."

"He ought to go into public health," said Vincent. "And start on her."

"Look," Guido said. "Take Jane. Jane was very decorative and all, but she came in late, left early, didn't come in on nice days, and sulked all the time. Besides, she was always on the phone and she took three-hour lunches. Furthermore, she couldn't spell, she lost five manuscripts, and she was cranky and rude. Now Betty Helen, on the other hand, is always on time, leaves on time, spells like a dream, knows grammar, and she only makes one phone call a day and it takes under four minutes. I think it's to her husband."

"I think she's a holy terror. You just wait," said Vincent. "Jesus, who would marry her?"

There were very few people Vincent liked. He liked Guido, whom he had known all his life; he liked his sister, who lived in Colorado; he had kind memories of a girl he had been engaged to; and he liked a girl who worked at the Board of City Planning. Her name was Misty Berkowitz. Vincent had discovered her one morning slumped over her typewriter, stirring her coffee in a desultory fashion with her fountain pen. Small oval spectacles slipped down her nose. She had amber-colored hair that fell into her eyes. She looked bored and misanthropic and was drawing mustaches on the faces in *The New York Times*. Vincent said good morning to her and was about to begin a conversation about the headlines when she looked up and growled: "Get the hell away from me." Later she came into his office to apologize. "It's hell in the morning," she said. Vincent felt his heart melting like hot candles. He asked her to have lunch with him and took her to a badly lit Italian restaurant.

Misty Berkowitz was twenty-five. She wore an elderly suede jacket and revealed to Vincent that she spoke German, French, and Xhosa.

"Xhosa?"

"I learned it in linguistics class. When I get enough money to get out of this dump, I'm going to go where they speak it and speak it."

"Where *do* they speak it?"

"I don't know. Africa or someplace. I never asked."

"Is Misty your real name, or is it short for something?" Vincent asked.

"It's real," she snarled.

"How did you get a name like that?"

"Because my mother is a jerk."

The waiter brought two plates of Fettuccine Alfredo. Misty ate daintily, as if her food were under a microscope. Vincent ate quickly, waiting for Misty to say something, but she was too involved in her pasta to speak. When the plates were finally taken away, she looked deeply and silently into her coffee cup.

"Are you a secretary or what?" he asked. "I mean, what do you do at your job?"

"What is this, Twenty Questions? I just sit around."

"Well, who do you work for?"

Misty tapped on her coffee cup with a spoon. "Some guy named George something. The guy with the pink glasses. You know the one. He has those hokey patches on his elbows. I never found out what his last name is. He comes around when he needs me and gives me stuff to analyze and edit. The rest of the time I sit around and read."

"How long have you been working here?"

"About six months, but I used to be on another floor. What do *you* do, anyway?"

"Garbage."

"That's clever. Garbage what?"

"I do studies of how much garbage is produced and how you can get rid of it. Right now I'm working on a method of compressing it into tubes that turn it into mulch."

"How inspiring," said Misty. "I think people should hate their jobs, because work is degrading."

Vincent tipped his chair back. He wondered if he could provide Guido with Misty Berkowitz to replace Betty Helen Carnhoops. That way, Guido would have an interesting and appealing secretary and Vincent could develop his connection with Misty. If she worked in Guido's office, Vincent could demonstrate to her what a fine, competent, and gentle person he was. Guido's office brought out the best in him, he felt. It occurred to him that he was going to fall in love with Misty Berkowitz, but he thought she found him affected.

"Rich people make me sick," she said.

Guido was brooding. Yesterday Vincent had been brooding. "We are on the verge of our lives," he had said despondently to Guido.

"What the hell does that mean?"

"We're prime. We're in the prime of life. We should be doing concrete, long-lasting adult things. It's terrible, but I still feel like a child. Every adult is the headmaster and I'm just about to be suspended. Why do I do these useless things, like hang my heart around Misty Berkowitz's neck? It's just like high school and here I am, walking around in an adult skin."

From time to time Guido was mentioned by his acquaintances as being "recently eligible," which caused him considerable distress. He had now been separated from his wife, the former Holly Stergis, for four months. She called from the country once a week and they met for lunch every two weeks, but Holly refused to have dinner with him. "It's too explosive," she said.

"I'm not going to be undone by you, or anyone like you," said Guido to himself. He was having a conversation in the mirror and his reflection was the former Holly Stergis. On good days, he made plans for their mutual future together, and on bad days he felt himself permanently severed from all human warmth.

Betty Helen Carnhoops appeared at the door. "Your friends are here," she said, in a tone that would have been appropriate to an announcement of botulism or the plague.

Vincent walked in, leading Misty Berkowitz by the elbow. He introduced her to Guido. His face was shining and hopeful. "Isn't this a nice office?" he said eagerly.

"Nice enough," mumbled Misty. "You do something literary, don't you?" Guido handed her a back issue of *Runnymede*. She shuffled the pages like a deck of cards.

"Would you like some Seltzer?" asked Guido.

"I'd like to put my feet up, or would it tarnish these gleaming surfaces?" said Misty. Guido provided her with a wicker basket and she put her feet up on it. She wore small, expensive green shoes.

"Would you like some Seltzer?" Guido asked again.

"I don't suppose you have anything as banal as coffee," said Misty.

'I'll ask my secretary to make some," said Guido.

"That awful girl outside? Jesus Christ, harlequin glasses. Will they never learn?"

"She's actually very pleasant," said Guido.

"I'd like some coffee, but not if I have to deal with her," Misty said.

"I'll get it," said Vincent, leaping out of his chair. "There's a delicatessen downstairs." He raced out of the office.

"You," said Guido to Misty, "are you and Vincent friends because you're both so negative?"

"Who's negative?" said Misty. "Besides, Vincent's not my friend. I don't even know him. I don't even know what I'm doing here."

"That's three negatives in a row," Guido said.

Vincent came in with the coffee, which was leaking through its paper bag. He handed it to Misty. He was positively wiped out by love.

Betty Helen Carnhoops was like a reef of calm in a bad storm. She functioned as smoothly as a hospital kitchen. Vincent said she was a vacuum cleaner made flesh. Her telephone voice was brisk and astringent. Her letters were little miracles: she justified each line like a veritype machine. She never spoke to Guido except in the line of work and her few conversational attempts were confined to such soothing and uninteresting subjects as the weather, or what time the window washer was coming in. However, she announced anyone who came to the office by buzzing Guido and telling him his friends had arrived. She announced in this way the window washer, authors, trustees of the Magna Carta Foundation, messengers, telephone repairmen, and delivery boys from the delicatessen. Guido had not noticed this. It was pointed out to him by Vincent.

"Betty Helen is so level. It's a pleasure," Guido said.

"That woman is lobotomized," said Vincent. "She's just waiting to strike. She's a menace. Why does she announce these Western Union messengers as your friends?"

The office hummed efficiently. For Guido it was like living in a quiet tunnel, safe and comfortable. The telephone and typewriter purred. Holly called to tell Guido that she was going to France with her mother for a few weeks and to cancel their lunch date. She called while Betty Helen was out to lunch, and after hanging up Guido put his head on his desk and fell into a short, miserable sleep.

That afternoon, Vincent proposed to Guido that he fire Betty Helen and hire Misty Berkowitz.

"She's very smart and she hates her job," Vincent said. "I think she would really like to work here, and she'd be around, see."

"For God's sake," snapped Guido, looking haggard. "Leave me with my Betty Helen Carnhoops. I can't take it any more."

"Take what any more?"

"I want to have some ordinary, stable person around and that's what I have. I am sincerely tired of having these beautiful flash girls running around being illiterate and ruining my life."

"Misty isn't illiterate, and she isn't beautiful."

"She's interesting-looking," said Guido. "And that's a bad sign."

"Anyway, she's not ruining your life. She's ruining mine," Vincent said.

"Don't be so melodramatic. If what you wanted was some nice, stable girl, that's what you'd have. You obviously don't want that or you wouldn't be hanging around with her."

"Don't moralize at me. She hates me. I'm sure she does. She told me that people like me were irrelevant. She says I don't do anything that doesn't feed the system. She says if there's a revolution I'll be useless. God, it makes me sad."

"If there's a revolution, that girl will have to give up her expensive green shoes. Besides, if you're so irrelevant, what's *she* doing with you?"

"I don't know. She gave me dinner the other night. It was pot roast. God, it's sad."

"Don't be so adolescent," said Guido. He was thinking of Holly.

"If you would only hire her, my life would be one solid round of bliss."

"And my life would be one solid round of hell. It's out of the question."

"She really hates me," said Vincent. "I'm sure of it."

One afternoon Vincent called Guido to ask if he and Misty Berkowitz could meet at Guido's office. Misty arrived first, wearing her green shoes and suede jacket. She put her feet up on the wicker basket and drank a bottle of soda.

"I don't mean to pry," Guido said to her, "but why are you giving Vincent such a hard time?"

"You guys," snickered Misty, "I haven't seen anything like you since junior high school. You're like thirteen-year-old girls."

"You have to admit you're not very nice to him."

"Why should I be? He has an easy life. Part of my function is to give him a hard time. It makes him feel alive." She twirled her shoe around on the tip of her toes. "He gets what he deserves, and he gets what he wants. We all do."

"People your age seem to have a very tough attitude."

"Tough Schmough. Don't be so patronizing."

"He says you hate him and string him along and won't go to bed with him."

"I might, if it's any of your business."

"Might what?"

"Go to bed with him."

"Then you *do* like him."

"I might go to bed with him if I get bored not going to bed with him." She yawned, showing small white teeth. The bottom row was slightly crooked.

"I think you have very rigid values, Misty. Life is very short and God knows it's difficult enough. If you like Vincent, you shouldn't be so awful to him. It's easier to be kind to people than is commonly believed."

"How Rabbinical," said Misty. "It's not all that easy. Even if I did like Vincent, I'd never let him know. People shouldn't know I like them. It gives them the upper hand."

"What a difficult girl you are," said Guido. He looked mystified and pained.

"Could be," said Misty, looking at her shoe. "Listen," she said. "Vincent thinks that he can be nice to me the way he's nice to everyone else. But he can't be, see, because I'm not everyone else, and I'm waiting for him to find that out."

"That's the first humane thing I've heard you say."

"The trouble with you rich people is you're polite all the time."

They sat silently for a while, listening to the dulled clicking of Betty Helen at the typewriter.

"What are you going to do about her?" Misty asked.

"You mean Betty Helen."

"Is that her name? Are you going to sack her?"

"Certainly not. Why should I?"

"Because she's obviously the most disgusting person in New York. Vincent says it *says* a lot about you that you hired her. He says she's a reaction against Holly Whatever and that hiring her is your attempt to regain some warped notion of stability."

Betty Helen buzzed on the intercom. "Your friend is here."

"I'm a little tired of that girl being made into a symbol of my being," said Guido.

Vincent walked to the door of the office. He looked shy and boyish and tripped on the door ledge.

It was eleven o'clock and Vincent was very sad. He had not been to his office at the Board of City Planning and was loitering around Guido's office eating shrimp bisque out of a can.

"I don't believe I've ever felt this awful," he said.

"What's your problem?" said Guido.

"Misty and I had a fight. I don't know what I've done wrong. Last night she threw a magazine at me and said I treat her like a stranger on the subway. I just don't understand. Then she said she didn't like anyone."

"She always says that," said Guido, who was going over a set of galleys with a blue pencil.

"This time she meant me. What did I do? I don't think I treat her like a stranger on the subway. I'm in love with her."

"Why don't you find some nice pleasant girl, for a change?" mumbled Guido over his pencil.

"*I* find some nice pleasant girl for a change. You go find some nice pleasant girls and look what *you* turn up! Holly Stergis and that thing outside. Nice pleasant people for Christ's sake."

"You shut up about Holly," said Guido. "You shut up about Betty Helen. At least I don't go panting off after some little kid who mistreats me."

"As far as I can see, neither of those two treat you at all. As far as I can see, *you're* the stranger on the subway."

Guido sighed and went back to his galleys. The former Holly Stergis was a source of constant unhappiness to him. Late at night, he spoke to her in his mirror. She was staying with her mother at the George Cinq in Paris and he had written her several letters. In return she had written him one postcard, which said: "I'm thinking all the time. I got your letters. Don't expect me to write because I'd rather talk. H." This postcard had filled him with nervous joy and expectation. Did it mean she was thinking about him? About them? Or did it mean that she wouldn't write because she was coming back to ask for a divorce? It seemed to Guido that he would not rest or calm or ease until he saw her, but she had neglected to say when she was coming back.

Betty Helen appeared at the door. "Your friend is here," she said. The friend turned out to be a delivery boy carrying three bottles of Seltzer. Vincent and Guido drank a glass each. They were both restless and edgy.

"Why don't you write another garbage study?" Guido asked.

"I'm in the middle of one but I can't keep to it. I sit in that bloody misshapen coat closet over at the Board and all I do is think about Misty. She says I'm putting myself through my own hoops, whatever that means. She actually *threw* a magazine at me. It was one of those thick ones."

"Be glad she didn't hit you with the telephone book," said

Guido. The sky darkened and it began to rain. Vincent read *The Wall Street Journal* and Guido read the *Times*. He told Betty Helen that he was out, if anyone should call.

Vincent and Guido sat in Guido's office. A member of the board had been visiting with a cigar and the window was open to clear the air. It was noon and they were eating pastrami sandwiches.

"Holly called this morning," said Guido. "She's back from Paris and she says we should see each other."

"What prompted it?"

"Nothing. She did it all herself." He flicked his finger against a glass bowl, which gave off a little ping.

"Are you going to see her?"

"I'm going to take her for dinner at the Lalique, which is where we always used to go, and sit at our old favorite table and I'm going to order smoked salmon and Châteaubriand and peaches in wine because that's what she likes and then I'm going to give her a bag of those lemon candies she likes from that place on Liberty Street because she's probably too lazy to go there herself."

"And why are you making these grandiose gestures?"

"Because it's time for me to straighten things out. I'm tired of being alone. I'm tired of being estranged and separated. I want it all back again."

"Supposing she doesn't?"

"She has to," said Guido grimly. "I really can't go on."

"I'm off to my garbage," said Vincent sadly. "Give Holly my love, will you. I'd love to see you back together."

"How's Misty coming along?"

"I'm going to see if she'll condescend to have lunch with me today. God, my life is shabby. Sometimes I think it's love and sometimes I think it's sickness. Life really *is* as complicated as she says it is. Except for people like Betty Helen, of course." Vincent and Guido looked at each other. For an instant they were twins, slightly exhausted by hope.

Betty Helen's eyeglasses glittered in the light as Vincent walked out. He mumbled goodbye to her.

Vincent was walking toward Misty Berkowitz's apartment. They had gone to lunch together and she had delivered a tirade at him, telling him that he was lacking in feeling, that he had no emotional life, that he was a typical polite rich person, and that if all it took to make him happy was for her to be polite back to him, he was a hopeless moron. He felt as if twenty magazines were hurled at him. Then he said: "I'm sorry, Misty. I am the only way I know how to be. It's senseless for me to tell you how fond I am of you because you don't believe me." He was about to slink off like a hurt dog, but she tugged on his sleeve.

She actually grinned at him. "Will you come over tonight and let me cook supper for you?"

"Would it make any difference?" he asked, miserably. She gave him a large, open, bright smile.

"That remains to be seen," she said, and kicked him gently on the ankle with her shoe.

Walking down the street he thought he heard a violin. It was followed by an oboe and a flute. Two more steps and he heard a bassoon and a cello. For a moment he thought he was hallucinating. As he walked farther the music got closer. He passed a brownstone with large open windows. A girl with a violin in her hand looked out onto the street. Behind her were a group of men and women holding oboes and flutes and bassoons and clarinets and violas, walking around tuning up. The notes scraped against one another. A plaque on the brownstone read: The Horton Little Symphony Society. Someone played a piano trill. The girl in the window looked at Vincent, smiled, picked up her violin, and began to play the opening bars of the Kreutzer Sonata. He smiled back and rushed down the street. He felt moved and foolish to find that there were tears in his eyes.

"Betty Helen quit today," said Guido. "Her husband is going to Oklahoma to study with someone called Mezzrobian. Did you ever hear of anyone called Mezzrobian? It sounded like someone everybody's heard of."

"There isn't anybody called Mezzrobian. There isn't even a Mr. Betty Helen Carnhoops. Jesus, who would marry her?"

"Well, she's gone. She had to go pack for the movers. Now I have to start this gavotte all over again. I suppose you'll start nagging me about Miss Berkowitz."

"No," said Vincent brightly. "She says she'll stay at the Board and see how we go."

"What does that mean?"

"It means how we work out together."

"Women are very strange," said Guido. "Even if they do what you want them to, they're not understandable."

"How's Holly?"

"She's looking for a new apartment for us. She says the old one is filled with bad vibrations and we should start out fresh."

"So you're back."

"Everything's back. Do you think you could write a poem about garbage? I have a page open."

Vincent sat with a sheaf of papers on his lap. "I have to get this thing in to *Urban Affairs Dialogue* by Friday."

On the desk, the glass bowls twinkled. No one answered the telephone on the first ring. No one typed behind the potted palm. Magna Carta Employment, a part of the foundation that found jobs for nonprofit agencies, was sending over some new girls tomorrow for interviews.

Guido corrected proofs. Vincent read his garbage study. They worked in silence for two hours. Then they both got up. Vincent had to meet Misty Berkowitz for lunch, and Guido had to meet Holly to look at an apartment. They paced around the quiet office for several minutes. Now that everything was back, they both felt dizzy and misplaced, like dancers after a long ballet.

 # passion and affect

Guido Morris and his wife, the former Holly Stergis, had been separated for almost six months, during which time Holly read the Larousse *Gastronomique,* went to France with her mother, and wrote Guido one vague postcard which did not explain why their present living arrangement suited her, or why she had thought of it in the first place.

One day, shortly before the six-month mark, she called from her parents' house in the country to say that she felt they ought to have dinner and talk things over.

"I think I've arranged my mind," she said.

It was a brief, explosive meal. They met at the Lalique, an obscure, ornate restaurant that had been the partial scene of their courtship, but neither of them had much in the way of appetite. They left their dinner virtually untouched but drank two bottles of white wine. Holly stared at her glass and said, "This place is littered with memories." Then they left abruptly, overtipping. At their apartment, the chamber of Guido's recent solitude, they decided to resume their life together.

"But we have to move," said Holly, with whose wardrobe Guido had cohabited silently for months. "I don't think we should live amongst our separateness."

73

"I'm not at all sure what that means," Guido said.

"It means that this is where we started, and this is where things didn't work out. Besides, I never liked the kitchen."

"I'm not at all sure why you left in the first place," said Guido. "You never said you didn't like the kitchen."

"I told you why I left," said Holly. "I needed time to be alone with myself and now I have. I thought it would be a profitable emotional experience for both of us." She propped her neck with one of the ornamental bed pillows she had resurrected from the closet, where Guido, who had not been able to look at them without pain, had put them.

"Holly, did I do something wrong? Are you, I mean, were you in love with someone else? I mean, did I have anything to do with this?"

"I worried about you," said Holly.

"So did I," Guido said grimly. They were silent for a while and then Holly turned over with the little sigh that indicated she was asleep.

Thus, their reconciliation. Holly was back, but even with her sleeping next to him, Guido turned over and over again during the night to make sure she was actually there. She always was, her hair nestled against the pillows and one elegant foot on top of the blanket. She was sleeping the sleep of the just and innocent. .Her clothes were neatly folded over the armchair that had held nothing for the past six months but copies of *The New York Times*. While Holly slept beautifully away, Guido slept fitfully, dreaming of lizards and relief maps of Brazil.

The next morning, she was up before him. He found her drinking coffee and wearing his old camel hair robe. What she called her "essential clothing" was still in the country. Her dark, thick hair was only slightly disarranged by sleep and her eyes were bright with unfocused alertness. She was reading the society page. At his place was a covered plate of eggs and bacon. She read to him from the paper, as if they had never been parted.

"Do you know Phillip Lamaze?" she said.

"No. Should I?"

"It says here that he was in your class at college and that he's just been named curator of the Rope Collection."

"What's that? Photos of hangings?"

"A gift of Mrs. Henry Rope. It's Chinese porcelain." She poured herself another cup of coffee, and Guido, who was generally teetotal, found himself wanting a drink. He had the feeling he would see Holly and die, so he barricaded himself in back of the sports page.

"I'm going to look for an apartment today," Holly said. "I've done the real estate page, and I made a whole bunch of calls before you got up." With that, she dismissed him. He kissed the top of her head, the only part of her accessible to him since she was deeply engaged in the movie review.

"I'll call you at lunchtime," she said.

Guido put on his tie and left. Walking down the stairs, he felt as if his knees were a pair of smashed artifacts from the Rope Collection and reflected that in matters of the heart, Holly was very businesslike.

It was a bright, strident autumn morning, of the sort Guido hated. The weather was not in correspondence with his mood: the sun shone through fat, white clouds, wind blew the leaves off the trees, and the sky was an intense, cheery gray. Guido was ripe for blizzard, or torrential rain. He walked to his office feeling dazed and weak-headed. His office housed the literary end of a foundation called The Magna Carta Trust, which he had inherited and which gave money to worthy artists with noble plans for large-scale cultural events. From his office, Guido dispensed money to colleges and poets, and novelists from Guam and Uganda. He also produced and edited the foundation's literary magazine, *Runnymede*. It was a sensible and elegant production, and in the seven years of Guido's editorship, had begun to turn over quite a tidy profit, a fact that caused considerable astonishment to the trustees.

Since he could not bear to think of Holly, whose return was

more like a collision than an event, he thought about his secretarial problems. The girl who had worked for him, Betty Helen Carnhoops, had quit to go to Oklahoma with her husband. She was a dull, efficient, and unattractive girl, as bland as cream of rice and probably as stable.

At the door to his office, he was greeted by a young man wearing his hair in the manner of John Donne, a three-piece suit, and cowboy boots.

"Can I help you?" Guido said.

"Yeah. I'm looking for Guido Morris."

"I'm Guido Morris."

"Well, I'm Stanley Berkowitz and I'm your new secretary."

"Did the temporary agency send you over?"

"No, my cousin did. Misty Berkowitz. The girlfriend of your friend Vincent Cardworthy."

"I've never had a male secretary before," said Guido.

"I'm not a secretary, man. I just type very fast. I just got out of Princeton and I used to be a speed freak. I'm in classics."

"A speed freak?"

"Yeah," said Stanley. Seeing Guido's blank face he said gently, "How old are you?"

"Thirty-four."

"Well, man," Stanley said. "A speed freak is someone who does ups, you know, methadrine, amphetamines. You must have read about it in the local media."

"I see," said Guido. "What's it like?"

"It's hell, man," Stanley said. "It turns your brain into pea soup."

"I've never had a speed freak for a secretary before."

"You don't now. I'm an ex-speed freak, but I'm a very nervous type, see."

"How nice for you," Guido said. "Can you take dictation?"

"No, man. I just write very fast 'cause I'm a nervous type, like I said."

Stanley wrote a rapid, legible hand. He made the coffee and spent two hours taking dictation. Shortly before lunch, he presented Guido with a stack of typed letters. All the "w's" had been left out and were beautifully written in by Italic pen.

"Is the "w" key on that typewriter broken?" Guido asked.

"No, man. It's a little device I made up to keep from freaking out. See, you choose a letter and then you leave it out and then you write it in. I started it when I was writing term papers, see. It's a little sanity device."

"It looks very nice," Guido said.

"Well, it looks like the key is broken, see, but it gives a sort of personal touch. Besides, I hate to type. It makes me edgy."

Guido's office was a long, stylish L. The prints on the walls were mostly Dürers, chastely framed in gilt wood. His desk was mahogany and seemed to have been made by a hinge fanatic. There were brass hinges on the sides, nailed into the front, and on the drawers. It was large enough to take a nap on.

The windows looked over the roofs of mid-Manhattan and Central Park. On a shelf that ran the length of the wall were back numbers of *Runnymede* and books by authors subsidized by the foundation or published in the magazine. On a long table was the collection of Peking glass bowls left to Guido by his Newport aunt. There was a brass watering can filled with eggshells and water, a combination suggested by Holly to give his plants a better life. Every morning, Guido watered the hanging fern, the geraniums, the grape ivy, and the potted palms behind which Stanley now sat. In the hall connecting the outer and inner offices was a little refrigerator made of bird's-eye walnut that when opened contained several cans of shrimp bisque, bottles of Seltzer, and a plastic lime.

At lunchtime, Vincent Cardworthy appeared. He was Guido's oldest and closest friend and, by quirk of good fortune, second cousin. They were both tall and lean. Guido was dark and Vincent was ruddy, but they both had happy, boyish, slightly haunted faces.

Vincent's office at the Board of City Planning was several

blocks from Guido and he frequently walked over for lunch. It was at the City Planning Board that he had fallen in love with Misty Berkowitz, who disapproved of Guido and Vincent with equal venom. Vincent was a free-lance statistician whose special field of expertise was garbage removal and disposal. "I'm in garbage," he often said but was forgiven, as his studies on the subject were considered to be quite brilliant. They were quoted in *The New York Times,* and republished in a large number of urban journals.

He found Stanley eating a pastrami sandwich behind the potted palm.

"What's happening on the rubbish heap?" said Stanley, by way of greeting.

"How's the life of a male secretary?" Vincent said.

"It's pretty far out," said Stanley. "I was just reading a little Homer here to get my mind uncoiled."

Vincent found Guido sitting at his desk drinking a glass of lime and Seltzer and reading a manuscript.

"What's happening on the rubbish heap?" he asked Vincent.

"Is Stanley writing your material now?" Vincent said. "How's Holly?"

Guido felt a surge of despair. "She's wonderful. I'm terrible. I feel as if I had been flattened by a truck, but she's as adaptable as a thermostat so she's happily reading the paper. She wants to move. She says we shouldn't live in the scene of our separation."

"I'm not at all sure I know what that means," Vincent said.

"It means that that's where we started and that's where things didn't go right. She said something last night about the artifacts of dissatisfaction. I can't talk about it. All I know is she's back, and that's what I wanted. It would be nice to know on what terms, but that doesn't seem to interest her."

"If Misty didn't hate your part of town so much, I'd take your apartment, seeing as mine is stereotypic and banal. Your part of town, according to her, is filled with uptight gentiles and rich people."

"Maybe one of these days we'll all be poor and happy." They exchanged a look of mutual exhaustion.

"I'm going to ask her to marry me," Vincent said. His eyes were slightly glassy.

"Why don't you stick your head in a coal stove? It saves time."

"I love her," Vincent said. "I know she loves me, but she won't say because she says I don't deserve to know."

"Isn't life simple," said Guido bitterly.

"In the old days," Vincent said, "I'd pop the question and she'd say yes and we'd go and do it. Then we'd settle down and live our lives. Everything would be as it should be."

"In the old days, there weren't any Mistys, or Hollys either. I don't think I know any more how things should be."

"Well, I'm just going to go ahead on the theory that things are the way they're supposed to be, and I think that Misty and I should get married."

"I'll send you the name of a good divorce lawyer for a wedding present," Guido said.

Misty Berkowitz was a small-boned girl with a long stride. Her hair was the color of amber and she wore wire-rimmed glasses. She was an assistant structural theorist at the Board of City Planning, where she had met Vincent. In the spring and summer she wore an old green suede jacket and in the winter she wore an old green suede coat. She had not intended to stay at the Board of City Planning: she wanted to go to the École des Hautes Études to study linguistics, but she had met Vincent and put it off. Vincent knew she had been planning to go abroad, but he had no idea that she had put it off because of him. Vincent was everything Misty disapproved of, and since she felt he was a blockhead, she had no intention of telling him anything.

She did, however, tell herself quite a lot of things, and one of the things she knew was how she felt about Vincent. No matter

what she said aloud about him—things that were generally savage
—she knew him to be a level, good-tempered, and intelligent person, deeply affectionate, but a man who knew as much about the
life of the emotions as an infant knows about parachuting.

Misty and her cousin Stanley did not frequent
each other, but since he had come East to college, a loving ani-
mosity had sprung up between them. Basically, they met at times
of personal crisis, and the last time Misty had seen him, he had
been miserably stewing over a girl called Sybelle Klinger who
could not make up her mind whether or not to share his sublet
with him. She had finally said yes, and Misty and Stanley had not
had any reason to get together.

When Misty called him, he assumed that it was a time of emer-
gency, so they met in the park and ate hot dogs at the zoo. Stanley
was family, and he was smart. His father and Misty's were labor
lawyers in Chicago. They got right down to cases.

"What do you think of Vincent?" Misty said. They were standing at the seal pool.

"I think he's a straight dude, man."

"Oh, knock it off, Stanley. I want to know what you think."

"I like him a lot. I mean, viscerally. But then, I haven't been
around him much." He watched the seals with envy. "That's the
way to live," he said.

"Do you think I should marry him?"

"I don't know from marriage," Stanley said. "Do you wanna?"

"Why can't you be serious?" Misty wailed.

"Don't get all worked up," Stanley said. "I need another hot
dog. You should marry him if you love him, right?"

"You are a rude, selfish little pig, Stanley."

"No I'm not, man. I'm just saying that if you love him, you
should do it to it."

"Isn't life simple."

"Yeah, man, it probably is, but not for weirdos like us. Come
on, let's get another hot dog and go see the yak."

In the weeks that they had been back together, Guido heard Holly mention someone called Arnold Milgrim several times. Since she neither explained nor described him, Guido supposed that he had been Holly's lover, but when she began to speak about him with the disembodied reverence with which you refer to the very famous, he assumed Arnold Milgrim was someone universally known—a sort of prime source, and not Holly's lover at all. But still he was not sure, and he endured this form of self-torture for a week or so. Then, one morning, he looked meaningfully at the coffee pot and said: "Pour me some more of that Arnold Milgrim." By the end of breakfast, he had called nearly every object by this name.

"Where's my Arnold Milgrim?" He said menacingly, looking for his briefcase.

Holly then explained that Arnold Milgrim had been a student of her grandfather's and she had met him on her recent trip to France. He taught philosophy at Oxford, on loan from Yale, and was the author of *The Decay of Language as Meaning, The Automatic Memory,* and *Fishing in the Waters of Time,* which was about Hegel.

As the day progressed, it seemed to Guido that he was perhaps the only person alive who had not heard of Arnold Milgrim: Stanley had read *Fishing in the Waters of Time* and said it was far out. Vincent reported having seen Arnold Milgrim on television in London. Finally, Guido made the first telephone call he had ever made to Misty Berkowitz, who told him that she had read parts of *The Decay of Language as Meaning* and found it provocative, but basically silly.

Then the subject of Arnold Milgrim was dropped, because the artifacts of dissatisfaction were dispelled by a series of painters, plasterers, and paperhangers who invaded the apartment. Guido had always wanted to have a closet papered with a map of eighteenth-century Paris—it was one of his low-level fantasies—and Holly spent two weeks looking for wallpaper with the right map on it. Monkeys climbing blue poles decorated with green squash blossoms appeared in the guest bathroom. Soft coats of unnecessary white paint were spread on all the walls. Five strange-looking men appeared on a Friday to scrape, stain, and wax all the floors. The Persian rugs came back from the cleaners glowing richly. Two boys who looked vaguely like Stanley showed up and fixed the kitchen by putting up some chic and useful shelves.

Finally, the last dust cloth was taken up, the rooms no longer smelled of paint, the curtains swayed immaculately in the autumn breeze.

One Saturday morning, the postman delivered a very heavy cream-colored envelope addressed to Holly. It looked as heavy as a wedding invitation—but it was a letter from Arnold Milgrim to say that he was coming to New York with one of his students. Embossed in gold on top of the page was the seal of Halifax College, Oxford.

"This is the sort of paper they use when the Empress dies," Guido said to Holly, who fired off a reply, inviting Arnold and his student for dinner.

"Spear me another of those little Arnold Milgrims," Guido said, and Holly absently dropped an Irish sausage on his uplifted plate.

Arnold Milgrim called on a Tuesday afternoon, and at eight o'clock he appeared. To Guido he seemed to be the size of a bug and wore a suit the sheer smallness of which was touching. It looked as if it had been reduced to scale to fit a box turtle. His socks were the deep red of arterial blood and around his neck he wore a scarf long enough to wrap around an elephant's midsection. On his arm was a thin girl whose toast-colored hair was so tenuously arranged that Guido was afraid to shake hands with her. She was introduced as Doria Mathers and she appeared to be asleep.

Arnold Milgrim was bald and his face had the naked political sensuality found on busts of Roman generals. He wore round glasses and it was not odd to see him with such a tall, thin girl. They were both dressed to the nines, or some odd version of it.

Doria Mathers wore a long yellow knitted dress and stockings that matched Arnold Milgrim's socks.

By the time drinks were finished, Arnold Milgrim had given Guido an excerpt from his new book for *Runnymede*. It was on the subject of the new metaphysics and was titled "The Amorphous Cage". Doria, on the other hand, had not spoken, and although she said nothing and did not raise her eyes from the sight of her own knees, she was hardly a quiet presence. As she later said of herself: "I fill my own space with a kind of inaudible loudness."

Guido thought that perhaps she had invented a new form of communication, so he sat opposite her by the fireplace and said nothing. From time to time he filled her glass and she gave him a mysterious, vacant smile. Arnold had decided to divide his time equally between Guido and Holly, and, finished with Guido, he talked quietly with Holly on the sofa.

"Doria is my most extraordinary student," he said. "The sheer weight of her mind oppresses her. Sometimes she simply can't speak because the process of thought is too intense. She thinks she sees birch trees where there aren't any. Oxford does not compensate for a life spent in Blessington, Vermont. I think the birch trees are a metaphoric orientation for her."

After dinner, while Guido and Doria sat on the sofa in silent communion, Arnold Milgrim talked to Holly. He talked about the weight of Doria's mind and, to Holly, he appeared to be almost out of his senses with love, but on the other hand, it was rather like the deep love a researcher might have for an experimental pet. Doria had uttered one entire sentence, at dinner, over the quiche, which Holly felt was a meal appropriate for people who had been on planes. Doria said: "Jet lag is the true disease of the late twentieth century."

As the evening wore on, she became more and more disarranged. She had taken off her shoes, which lay one on top of the other on the floor. Her tenuous hair arrangement had dissolved completely, and Holly, whose neatness was like the sheen on an

Oriental pearl, could see that there was a lot to be said for dishevelment.

On his side of the room, Arnold Milgrim said to Holly: "Look at her shoes. She always leaves her shoes like that and when I see them and I think of the power of her intellect, it almost brings me to tears. Once I found her slip crumpled up into the shape of a heart." He sounded almost anguished. He asked Holly to show Doria around New York while he went to see his publisher. As they left, Holly asked Doria what she would like to see.

"I'd like to go to all the knitting shops," Doria said. "I love to knit. It's like playing chess for me."

Life was back to normal, sort of. Holly said: "Now that we've had one set of dinner guests, it's time to have Vincent."

"Vincent is part of a pair, now."

"I know, and I want to meet her. Besides, now that we're consolidated, I want to see how it feels in front of real friends."

"I'm not sure what that means."

"It means that we're really back together and it would be nice and tightening to throw it around in front of a crowd."

"It's murk to me." Guido said. "Besides, Vincent isn't a crowd. *Misty* is a crowd."

He looked at his beautiful wife, his beautiful apartment. Life had all the accoutrements of grace. Their communal mornings were brisk and affectionate, their nights rhapsodic and passionate, but Holly conducted herself like a bird of paradise that had flown through the window of a house in Des Moines and settled down. She did not bother to explain her presence, or the reason for their parting, or her reason for coming back. She was simply, solidly there. His happiness in her company made Guido forget to mention his great bafflement on these issues when he was alone.

He decided, in desperation, to maintain a policy of silence, and thus felt lurches in his heart when Holly so much as went around the corner for a bunch of parsley. Their separation had caused him severe underground pain, and he was constantly afraid that she would disappear.

He knew it would wear off, but when Holly returned from shopping or getting the mail, he felt he had been given the kiss of life, or a Vermeer for his very own.

The idea of dinner with Guido and Holly appalled Misty Berkowitz.

"I will not sit around in some palazzo making small talk over a garbagy rack of lamb."

"You're not getting rack of lamb. You're probably getting chicken and Holly wants to meet you."

"I will not be observed," shouted Misty. "I will not be checked out by a bunch of rich people. I will not be weighed on the heavenly scales and found wanting."

"Oh, Misty. How could you ever be found wanting? Guido likes you. I love you. How could anybody not?"

"That's an egocentric notion if I ever heard one," Misty said.

"I don't ask for much," Vincent said. "It's only dinner with Guido." He looked woebegone and puzzled.

Misty lived in a nice, breezy apartment, filled casually with books, records, and plants she watered only when they were ready to expire. She was sitting in a worn old chair with her leg over the arm. She got up suddenly and stomped over to the window. Vincent stood beside her and turned her gently toward him. Her eyes were filled with tears. His heart failed.

"Misty, what's wrong? It's only dinner." To his intense amazement, she put her head against his chest and wept onto his shirt.

He had known her for a year, and she had never cried in his presence, not even at the movies. He suspected that she cried in private, but her privacy was so private he could not know. She had kept their relationship light and bantering for a year, taunting him, torturing him, he often thought, and making him laugh. She never even snuffled. He was filled with awe and panic. A torrent of love swept over him with the force of a Japanese tidal wave.

"Do you know how much I love you?" he said into her hair.

"If you love me so much, give me a handkerchief."

He looked steadily at her.

"How can you be this way, Misty? How can you be so flip when I'm serious."

"You only get mushy when I cry."

"You never cried before," Vincent said.

"You think you're serious, but only when you want to be." She rifled his pocket and fished out a Kleenex.

"Misty, do you care at all for me? Do you *like* me?"

"Enough," she said. "More than you deserve." Then she pressed her head against the window and began to cry again. He took her into his arms, and asked her to explain.

"What the hell am I supposed to wear?" she sobbed. "Oh, God, this is awful." Vincent's knees buckled. He dried her eyes with his handkerchief, and when he asked her to marry him, she told him he was only asking because she had broken down and then she suggested a game of gin.

"If I win, will you marry me?" Vincent said. He shuffled the cards with professional aplomb.

"How can you be so flip when I'm serious?" Misty said, and ginned out after four picks.

The next day, in her office at the Board of City Planning, Misty surveyed what she had chosen for her lunch. The yogurt tasted like acrid library paste. The pear she had taken a bite of was abandoned in back of a cup of coffee; it was an unripe, unsweet, rocky little pear. She knew she was hungry, but her appetite had left her. She sat looking at the pear and thought of Vincent. Her left leg was cramped. She had the beginnings of a headache. She was suffering. She looked out the window into the soft fleecy sky and thought of Vincent again. Then she closed the door and tried unsuccessfully to cry. She knew all she had to know about Vincent: it was only a matter of time until the war of nerves she was waging played out. She knew she prized and loved him, and knew that she would continue to give him a hard time until the knowledge made real sense to her. She also knew that she treated him lovingly, but Vincent only understood loving gestures if they were accompanied by the kind of soppy utterance found in romance magazines. She never told him how much she loved him: after all, wasn't he an emotional retard? Wasn't he a cretin not to know how loaded every one of her gestures was? Wasn't she giving herself away daily for all the world, except Blockhead Cardworthy, to see?

Accused of nastiness, Misty said to Vincent: "If I expressed even a small amount of my tenderness, I'd be sobbing on your shoes at least eighteen hours a day. Don't you know when you've got a good deal?"

Her battle with Vincent was that he was worse than a blockhead, he was naïve and objective. She didn't want to be a girl he loved, she wanted to be understood: the girl who was loving Vincent was a complicated little scrapper, and when he realized that, she figured she might give him a break.

She piled the papers neatly on her desk and pulled on her coat.

Out on the street, she windowshopped, staring with rapt depression at rows of mannikins in glossy trousers. A mood of gothic desolation moved in on her, and out of pique she bought a silk shirt she could not afford, and a recording of C. P. E. Bach's cello concerto. Then she ambled over to a candy store she had hitherto only dared browse in front of, and went in to buy for Vincent a box of his beloved French *marrons*. When she was told the price of this item, she knew that reason had indeed deserted her.

Vincent found Misty in her tiny office.

"Guido says they want us tomorrow night for dinner."

It was early afternoon, and the sky was cloudy. Misty sat at her desk, bathed in the grayness, looking stricken.

"O.K.," she said, like a child acquiescing to a dentist's appointment.

They met after work and walked slowly downtown to Misty's apartment. She had been behaving oddly all week, quiet, sad, remote, and she had cried. The part of Misty Vincent usually lived with was raucous, sharp, and frequently heartrending, but this was heartbreaking.

He read the paper while she took a nap on the couch. He saw how tired and sweet and intelligent she looked, even sleeping. He thought he understood unhappiness, but he didn't know if this was it. When she woke up, she sat for a long time without speaking. Finally Vincent pulled the hassock up in front of her, and took her hands.

"Are you going to talk to me and tell me what's going on with you? I can't bear to see you this way."

She shrugged and held his hands tighter.

"Does it help if I tell you I love you, or does it make it worse?" he said.

Then she began to cry. It was the second time in two days, but its effect on him was not dampened by repetition.

"O.K.," she said. "This is it."

His heart seemed to stop. This was it. He felt a streak of instant desolation and misery.

"Not what you think, you sap," said Misty. "I just can't keep this up much longer. Sometimes I wonder if you know what I'm like, and sometimes I think you do. I'm just sick of keeping you at arm's length and not telling you anything. You have no idea how melodramatic I am. If you don't know that I love you, then you're God's own fool, but don't expect me to treat you the way you think girls in love are supposed to."

"I don't think you're remotely like anyone I've ever known."

"You think I'm bad to you, but I'm only bad to me, because I never believe anyone. When I'm not being nasty I don't have any equilibrium. You may find yourself hooked up to a real soap opera, if I let go. Will you like that?"

"I think I'd like almost anything," Vincent said.

They clasped each other in happiness and relief.

"I think we earned this," said Misty, who was in tears again.

"I think we did too."

They drank a bottle of champagne before dinner and then tied up the telephone for an hour calling the Berkowitzs in Chicago and the Cardworthys in Connecticut to announce their intentions.

When the champagne wore off, they were tired and headachy and they lay in bed in slight discomfort.

"Are you having second thoughts?" asked Misty.

"I'd be the happiest man on the planet if I didn't have a headache," said Vincent. "Are you?"

"I never have second thoughts," Misty said. "It's against my religion to have second thoughts or enter the city of Mecca."

At breakfast, Vincent appeared to have been almost demolished by joy, but Misty, on the other hand was back to normal. Having carried her love around like a guilty secret, she felt as well placed in the world as a fresh loaf of bread. Vincent saluted her with a glass of orange juice.

"Here's to our happy future," he said.

"Your optimism is truly record-breaking," said Misty.

"What's wrong with a happy future?" Vincent asked.

"This is the twentieth century," said Misty. "Not hardly the great age of happy futures." She kissed him behind his ear. Vincent made the coffee.

"There are happy futures for some," he said.

"You and your debutante fantasies," she said, turning onto his plate a perfect omelet.

Holly had promised to show Doria around New York, and they hit every knitting shop in town, until Holly thought she would overdose at the sight of another skein. Doria bought seven pairs of knitting needles and several pounds of wool. She shopped briskly, but otherwise she was a study in manifest chaos.

Holly was impeccable: she had not opted for neatness, it had been thrust upon her by nature. She had simple, unadorned features, and thick straight hair that fell unalterably to her shoulders. Clothes on her looked somehow cleaner and more starched than they did on other people.

Doria Mathers wore a dress of angora that had both shrunk and stretched. The heel of her left shoe looked as if it might break off at any moment. Her hair, after a day buying wool, looked frenzied, but decorative. She was possibly the world's sloppiest knockout.

During lunch, Holly learned that Doria had been tutored at home, and in the process had learned Hindi and Bengali. No one in her family was particularly interested in Indian studies, but they all felt it was good intellectual training. She said she was going to write a book called The Architecture of Chaos. Then she said that Arnold Milgrim was the greatest man she had ever met, and possibly the greatest man who had ever lived. They were to be married in the spring, when Arnold's divorce came through.

"Arnold says I am a person of deep and sudden petulance," she said.

That night, at dinner, Holly asked Guido if he thought she was a person of deep and sudden petulance.

"I think probably everyone in the world is except you," he said.

"Do you ever think things like that about me?"

"Certainly not."

"Doria told me that Arnold says that she's a person of deep and sudden petulance."

"That girl," said Guido, "is a person of deep and constant torpor, as far as I can see."

"I think it's a romantic thing to say," said Holly.

"I think Arnold Milgrim is a person of deep and frequent idiocy," Guido said.

"Our natures are often at variance," said Holly, over the peach mousse.

Guido threw his spoon down on the table.

"Goddamn it, Holly. You go off and leave me and can't get out a coherent sentence as to why, then you come back and don't explain yourself, and you want me to go around blathering about how you are a woman of deep and pensive magnetism. If you want someone who will make a poetic fetish out of each of your many qualities, go off with Arnold Milgrim and I'm sure his lady love will sleep through the whole deep and meaningful proceeding. Just being loved isn't good enough for you." With that he stormed into the library and brooded. He rarely lost his temper. To him it was like losing his keys, and he never did that either. When he was angry, he was a person he was not comfortable with, but as he sat in his armchair, he realized what righteous anger really was.

Holly stood meekly in the doorway. She was carrying a tray of coffee.

"I'm sorry," she said. "Sometimes you're so level I feel I ought to fluff up the pillows between us. You're the only person in the world I love. I think you're the finest person I've ever met. It frightens me."

He gave her a look of love and grief.

"Whatever," he said. "You are frequent hell to live with."

Vincent and Misty stopped at a florist on the way to dinner and bought Holly and Guido a large bouquet of snapdragons.

"It'll be nice, all of us together," Vincent said.

"Aren't you the happy boyscout."

"Oh, give me a break," Vincent said.

She took his arm and they kissed in the street. In the beginning of their relationship, Vincent had been disturbed by what he called public displays of affection.

"You think shaking hands on the street is risqué," Misty used to say to him.

Now Vincent found street-corner kissing one of the delights of life and it was Misty who had grown somewhat prim.

"Arnold Milgrim and his lady friend are coming for coffee," Vincent said.

"That Holly," said Misty. "If she doesn't watch it, she's going to be the Bonwit Teller edition of Madame Récamier."

At the door, there was affection all around. Vincent and Guido clasped each other on the back. Vincent kissed

Holly. Guido kissed Misty. Holly and Misty took each other's measure.

Misty and Vincent stood bashfully in the hall.

"We're getting married," Vincent said, which admission engendered another round of handshakes and kisses.

"Did you know that Arnold Milgrim's lady has run off with your cousin?" Holly said.

"Whose cousin?" Vincent asked.

"Misty's," said Guido. "Arnold and I were having a conference today, and Arnold brought Doria up with him. When we came out, Stanley and Doria had disappeared, and haven't been heard from. If she comes back, they're coming for coffee. Arnold and Doria, that is."

"I never thought of Stanley as someone you would run off with," Misty said.

After dinner, Arnold Milgrim and Doria appeared. She was looking more windblown than ever.

Holly, Vincent, and Arnold had brandy. Misty and Guido drank coffee and watched Doria knit on the couch.

"Stanley has the same last name as you," Doria said to Misty. "Is that common in New York, or is he kin?"

"First cousin," said Misty.

"Your cousin reads Greek divinely," Doria said sleepily. "He read Plato quite movingly. We spent the afternoon reading the Apology. Your cousin has very beautiful forearms."

Then she and Arnold left.

"I never noticed Stanley's forearms before," said Misty. "I'll have to check them out."

They finished another bottle of wine at the dining room table and talked about the wedding. Holly and Misty exchanged looks of genuine sweetness, looks that were rare for both of them. Holly said she hoped they would be friends, and Misty, a little wine-dazed, knew that affection and love were general, once they had been specified. In love with Vincent, she was willing, and almost helpless, to love Holly, Guido, the rugs on the floor, the postman, telephone operators.

"Misty thinks that all this institutionalizing of love makes you live outside the moral universe," Vincent said.

"She's right," Guido said. "I drink to the moral universe."

"I drink to Misty and Vincent," said Holly.

"I drink to Arnold Milgrim and my cousin Stanley," Misty said.

"I drink to a deeply wonderful life," said Vincent.

They clicked their glasses, and under the fragmented lights of the chandelier, they drank to a deeply wonderful life.

 # the man who jumped
into the water

DURING THE ONLY SERIOUSLY bad year of his business, Charlie Hartz bought the old Berkely house and installed himself, Flossie his wife, and their child Minna in it. It was an old, enormous house, built in the early 1900's by a local millionaire. It had gray gables, five fireplaces, oak paneling, leaded-glass windows, and fifteen rooms for the three of them to live in. At the time my parents met them, they were cramped into four of the fifteen rooms while plasterers, carpenters, electricians, and painters brought the house down and put it back together.

The next year, when his business was in better order and the house was complete, Charlie spent six months designing a swimming pool, and during the winter, when everyone said he was crazy to begin digging, Charlie and a crew of five dug, laid, and finished it. It was a bit shorter than a full-size Olympic pool, and it was very deep, except for a couple of yards at one end shallow enough for Minna, who was six, to learn how to swim, and for Flossie's friends—the "bosom dippers," Charlie called them—who were not up for serious swimming. It was said to be a miracle of construction, because of the angle and the slope and the fact that it was built between small swells in the ground. It had a bronze frog on one side that spat water, and the border and sides were inlaid with blue-and-white Mexican tiles with flowers on them, and that was miracle enough for me. After serious consultation with the diving pro at the country club, Charlie put in a low board and a high dive that was slightly lower than a standard high jump.

My sister and Charlie spent hours diving, to the horror of Flossie and my mother, who thought that constant diving would do something to their hearing and sinuses. My sister was the better diver. She dove like some sleek bird—or the way diving might be done in an ideal water world. Charlie was forty-two at the time, and getting vaguely soft, and he dove with a solemn clumsiness. He was very determined about it. They had a general competition to see who could do the fanciest dives, and a personal competition in which one would stand on the high board and one on the low. The object of this game was to see if they could hit the water at the same time. One of them would call out the name of a dive, and they would have to correct for the difference in height and spring. This amused them endlessly. My sister was twenty-one at the time, and sullen. Except for her beau, Willis, who was clerking for the D.A., Charlie Hartz was one of the few people she liked. Since I had just turned seventeen, we didn't have much to say to each other, and since neither of us had quite stopped battling our parents, we had nothing much to say to them. On Friday afternoons, Willis would appear at the pool, and Charlie, Flossie, my parents, Willis, and my sister would sit in the sun drinking gin-and-lime. Charlie had bought my sister her first drink in a restaurant, and she loved him for it.

We spent days at their pool. I would take charge of Minna, who was interested in learning how to blow bubbles underwater. She was moonfaced and diffident. I taught her to stand on her head in the shallow end. Charlie and my father would listen to the ball game on the radio and plan some complicated, technological project for the winter. Flossie and my mother would roast delicately in the sun, splash once or twice in the pool, and get the lunch. Usually in the afternoons, the Flowers would arrive after their golf game. My parents and the Flowers clung to some dried-out, age-old feud between them, and they were civil but not cordial. The atmosphere became intensely sociable and civilized. Ice clinked diminutively in glasses.

Jeremy was the Flowers' son. When I was thirteen and he was fourteen, we had met at Sunday school and fallen in love. This meant that we wrote precocious notes to each other and, thrown together at parties, escaped out side doors and kissed in garages. No one paid much attention to us until Jeremy was sixteen and got his driver's license. Then attempts at sabotage were made by both sets of parents, but we were still holding hands and running off in the car and coming home too late. He was going away to Dartmouth in September, and we spent the summer clinging to each other when we could and drugging ourselves into the numbness we thought would be helpful in the fall. That particular summer took on a klieg-light clearness. It was like sharp cutting glass, because we were on the edge of adolescent pain and loss.

One afternoon, when Flossie and my mother were in town shopping and my father was swimming laps underwater, Charlie dragged me over to the garage, where he had taken apart the engine of the lawnmower and had unsuccessfully tried to get it back together. It was damp and mossy in the garage, and wherever I stepped crankcase oil slicked on me. I handed Charlie a pair of pliers. He said, "Is your heart going to break when the White Hope goes off to Dartmouth?" That made me angry, and I left him to his motor. I thought he was condescending and insensitive. In the pool, I realized that he was the only person who had taken enough notice of me and Jeremy to comment, and I was very struck with that. From then on I watched him, and I noticed that when the Flowers showed up with Jeremy slouched behind, Charlie arranged it so that we were off together or with him, away from where the air was being punctured with icicles of politeness.

Jeremy at the time was a tall, gangling boy with slate-blue, stricken eyes. He had been too tall too young and had kept his defensive slouch long after he had grown out of the need for it. He was Scholar of the Year at his school, and got the Greek and Latin award and the prize for the best French poem, so Charlie called him the White Hope. He loathed his parents and tolerated mine, but years of social pressure had worn him down. When he was angry, his voice was an outraged whine, but usually it was blunted at its edges and came out as a smudgy hostile murmur. With Jeremy, Charlie was impatient and savage. He would cut through Jeremy's posed nastiness and drive him into actual fury. He said to me of Jeremy, "That punk's got a great future ahead of him if he can tell his parents to go to hell and someone doesn't knock him off for his affectations." I thought this was very revolutionary talk from a parent. He said to me, of me, "You're an all-right girl, but you should wear lipstick and not run around looking like some two-bit beatnik." I wondered why we took it, and we did because Charlie found some mutual ground between you and him, and fought an honest battle there. Besides, he swore in front of us and told us that our mothers were hysterical, and that generally goes over well with adolescents.

Charlie Hartz was a very ordinary-looking man. The few times I saw him in a suit, I was shocked at how much he looked like hundreds of men in suits. He was medium height, medium weight, and his hair was a medium cut—colorless dark brown that became spiky when wet. He had a trick knee, which made him sway slightly when he walked, and he wore the usual kind of black-rimmed glasses. He wore them when he swam, and for diving he had a piece of elastic that went around his head like an Indian band to keep them on. Flossie worried, but they never broke. My father said that Charlie took nothing seriously and that he played with his business, but it never occurred to me then that he was the only person I had ever known who knew how to play, and he put himself entirely into whatever he was doing. He rarely laughed, but when he did it was like a meal.

Toward the end of the summer, Charlie gave Jeremy and me a going-away present. He said to Jeremy, "I'm taking the family to New York for the weekend. Clean the pool, will you?" I was standing next to Jeremy, so he meant me, too. He threw us the keys to the gate and said, "Keep an eye on it." The pool was ours for the weekend. We decided on night swimming, which neither of us had ever done. Since our parents knew that Charlie had given us use of the pool, it was a sanctioned thing; if I came home late at night with wet hair, there was no need for explanations.

There were lights around the side of the pool, and behind heavy glass plates there were lights in the pool. We turned them all out and lit candles in glasses and picked some overripe roses and tossed the petals in. The air was cold and the pool was like a vast warm bath. "We should swim naked," Jeremy said. We sat on the edge considering this, our flesh puckered and dripping. Some moths had knocked themselves out on the candle glasses and were lying in little pools of water, beating the powder off their wings until they died. "Let's," he said. We were very shy about it. We took our suits off underwater and threw them to the side of the pool. The water folded over us. I had never been swimming at night and never been swimming naked, and I had never been naked with anyone before. We floated on our backs away from each other, testing how it felt. Then we played a few timid water games, ducking each other, to play out the strangeness of it. When we got out, it was cold and overcast. It was as if the water had mated us, and we dried each other with the solicitous tenderness of old couples. We became very modest, and dressed in the garage with our backs to each other.

The next day, we cleaned the pool and went swimming at night until it rained. On Sunday night, the Hartzes came back and gave an impromptu party. Jeremy and I had to put in an appearance but Charlie maneuvered us to the door and we escaped. We drove to the arboretum and threw stones into the pond. I said, "When we were swimming naked, what do you think they were doing?"

Jeremy said, "I don't care. Whatever they were doing, the others were thinking about it and Charlie was doing it."

Then the police cruised by and chased us out.

       The last week before Jeremy left for Dartmouth was very difficult. We felt as if a conspiracy of parents was keeping us apart, but the fact was that no one bothered to think we needed to be together, so he was kept busy shopping and I was kept busy with being busy. We escaped to the Hartzes' as a convenient refuge. That week it was cold, and no one would swim with Charlie except us. When it looked like rain, he would jump into the water and stay there until the lightning began, and Flossie would come from the house and scold him until he got out.

Suddenly Jeremy was packed and gone, my sister went back to college, and I hung around waiting for my last year of high school to begin. Jeremy and I wrote every day, and Jeremy's parents started complaining about the telephone bills he was running up calling me. There were two mild crises, and both involved Charlie Hartz.

First, Willis and my sister split up temporarily, and since she and my mother weren't speaking, I found out from Charlie one afternoon in October. He was keeping the pool open until it got really cold, and I would go and swim with him. After his lecture about how sloppy my backstroke was, he said, "Your sister and that lawyer fellow had a fight."

"How do you know?" I said.

"I'm not as out of it as you think," said Charlie. "She called me up at work and told me."

"What did you say?" I asked.

"I said that long-distance things like this either play out or she'll marry him. And by the way, how's the Dartmouth wonder?"

At the end of October, my sister and Willis became engaged and decided to get married after New Year's. It was all part of the winter's loss. My sister and I had never been close, but I was used to her being around as my sister, not as Willis's wife. At their engagement party, Charlie winked at me and said, "I told you so." I remember thinking how ghastly and prim he was, but what a good time he was having at it.

Then one afternoon Charlie called me up. "Come to my office. It's important. Your White Hope is here."

When I got there, Charlie met me at the door. He was impatient and put out. "Would you please tell Jeremy that he is *not* to quit school."

"Is that what he says?" I asked.

"He says that everyone up there is illiterate and no one has ever heard of Samuel Beckett. Is he the guy who wrote *Way of All Flesh?*"

"Samuel Butler," I said.

"Never read it," he said.

"What did you say?"

"I told him that he was an adolescent punk, so he's very pissed off. He doesn't understand that he needs something to put his intelligence into."

I was dispatched to Jeremy, and we sat on a leather couch necking. Charlie gave us half an hour; then he appeared with sandwiches and beer from the delicatessen. We discussed the alternatives to going back to school. One of them was working for Charlie, learning how to be a stockbroker. One was to live at home and fight with his parents. One was to travel without money and end up with mononucleosis. Jeremy decided to stay home for the weekend and go back to Dartmouth.

After he was gone, I thought about Charlie Hartz. It seemed that he was very bound up in my life, but apart from the summer and at my parents' dinner parties I rarely saw him. What kept people like me and Jeremy and my sister around him was that Charlie got the best out of what you were at the time you were it. Jeremy was a punk and I was a sloppy adolescent, and Charlie both savored our conditions and responded to what we were without any of the condescension adults usually fall back on. When he discovered that I could draw, he made me teach him and he spent several hours a day drawing pictures of Minna, which he would make me criticize. To pay me back, he became merciless about my backstroke, standing like a raja at the end of the pool, shouting insults until I got out of the water, blue in the face, and told him to go to hell. He arched an eyebrow. "If you were some sort of a spastic, I'd leave you alone. But if you tried you'd have a really poetic backstroke going for you." He didn't mind laziness, as long as it was not laziness about doing something. He pried out of Jeremy that Jeremy took pictures, and the two of them spent an afternoon in the New Jersey swamps taking artistic photos of swamp grass. It gave both of them fantastic head colds. When he found out that my father knew how to install telephones, splicing into the Bell lines, and thereby cheating the telephone company, he and my father put an antique phone in every room of the Hartz house, and when Flossie complained that the ringing was driving her crazy they figured out a way to shut off the ringing and silenced ten of the phones. With my sister, he went diving and did the crosswords. He got all the obscurities, like brass money of India and water birds of the South Seas, and she got all the puns.

As winter started, Flossie and her set began their serious socializing with the usual round of dinner parties. At this time, Charlie and some local boy built a little car out of old parts, which Charlie used as a golf cart-*cum*-Land-Rover, and he appeared at parties slightly oil-stained. The gate to the pool was locked, and there was a flat wooden roof fitted over it, so that if Minna managed to get through the gate she couldn't fall in. After the first snowfall, he took Flossie and Minna to Barbados for two weeks.

Right before Christmas the weather became unnaturally warm. Snow melted into mud and car wheels skidded in it. The sky and the ground were mud-colored; it was like living between two roofs. I came home from school one afternoon on the warmest day, and in the living room I found my sister, who was not due home for another week. She and my mother were drinking and they were both red-eyed. It was another crisis. I wondered if she and Willis had broken off the engagement. I hung up my coat and my mother met me at the closet.

"What's going on?" I said.

She was very tense. "Something's happened," she said.

"What?" I asked.

She said very quietly in a hysterical voice, "Charlie Hartz is dead."

It was shocking, and I stepped backward, away from her voice. "Why?" I asked.

She said, "He shot himself this morning in his car," and rubbed her knuckles against her teeth.

It was the first time anyone I knew had died. I tried to imagine what Charlie had thought of when he got into his car and when he put the gun up to his temple. I wondered what he felt when the bullet went through his head. I wondered what he felt now, dead, and where he was. Then I went to my room and cried. I wondered if it wasn't true at all and he was in his garage, working on his golf cart. When my father came home, he made me drink some brandy and then we went to Flossie's house. Minna had been sent to an aunt's, and Flossie was under sedation. Her mother was there, a keen-eyed, regal old woman, who had a foxlike intelligent face that prowed over an enormous bosom. She spoke to my parents off in a corner, and what I wasn't supposed to hear was that Charlie hadn't left a note, that his business was in order, and that, as far as they knew, his health was good. The rumors were that he was bankrupt or had cancer. But there was no note, no sign.

My parents stayed with Flossie's mother at Flossie's that night, and my sister and I went home. We were both dazed and kept mumbling "I don't believe it" at each other. She talked to Willis for an hour on the telephone. When we finally had dinner, it was as if the whole house was in the midst of a funeral. None of the lights seemed to work and we ate in dimness. We picked at our food. Willis came over and spent the night.

My parents came back the next morning and we sat at breakfast, all of us tired and strained. The telephone rang and my mother answered it. "It's for you," she said to me, frosty in the voice. "It's Jeremy's mother."

Mrs. Flower said how sorry she was to disturb me, that we all must be very upset. What she was calling about was that Mr. Flower had called Jeremy to tell him the news. He had taken it very badly and refused to come for the funeral. She wanted me to call and make him come home for it.

I called, and Jeremy said that he knew what he felt about Charlie and that his coming to the funeral wouldn't bring Charlie back and he refused to come down to hear someone who barely knew

Charlie reciting insincerities over his body.

I asked him if he would come home for me, because *I* had to go to the funeral.

"I won't watch those vultures socializing around him," he said. We were both very shaky. He said he would come down to see me, but not to go to the funeral. Then he said, "Did they tell you exactly what happened?"

"He shot himself," I said.

There was an odd sort of glee in his voice, like someone championing a defeated, finished fighter. "He got up, had breakfast, and drove his car off and did it," he said. "But that's not all. It's very corny."

I was furious. "What are you talking about?"

"It's corny," he said. His voice was ragged. He was very near tears. "Don't you know where he did it? He drove to Paradise Lane. *Paradise Lane.* That's very corny. He did it deliberately." He went on and on, about how Paradise Lane was the suicide note he didn't leave, and how it was an existential gesture. He was babbling and I was crying.

After I hung up, I asked my father if the bit about Paradise Lane was true.

He said it was.

"What do you think it meant?" I asked him.

He put his pipe in his mouth and looked at me with the sort of worldliness that spans humor and outrage. "Not a damn thing," he said. "Just a place to park his car."

 a road in indiana

R AD MC CLOSKY was born in 1938, Patricia
Burr knew. His hair is dark blond, he is six feet tall, and he
weighs in at one hundred and eighty-five pounds. At the age of
twenty-three he married the former June Hulton and was divorced
six years later. He has a son, Tyler, for whom he has written a
number of songs, including "Tow-Headed Angel." This information appears on the back of Rad McClosky's record album, *Closing Doors,* and it is from this source that Patricia Burr also knew
that Rad McClosky had been a delivery man with the Tina Laundry in Nashville before he was discovered singing with Farron
Leeds and the Neap Brothers, as one of the Neap Brothers. Patricia had never heard music like this until she got to Indiana, where
the air waves were pulsating constantly with it. During the day,
when Richard was teaching, she played the record over and over,
learning the songs by heart. At night, and in the shower, she
hummed the title song. When the record was playing, she sang
with it:

"The lights went out when you walked out on me
Closing doors is all that I can see
Now my heart is dark and shuttered and
My windows painted shut
At night I cry for what can never be."

The first day she had the record, Patricia played it for Richard, who sat smoking his pipe and listening intelligently, hunched in his chair with his elbows on his knees. When it was over, she looked at him hopefully. He thought for a minute and then asked her if she would mind not playing it when he was at home.

Rad McClosky was Patricia's only happy discovery in Indiana. She had been there a year, but she had been an Easterner all her life, and she was a stranger. One afternoon, driving home from the Great West Supermarket, she punched randomly at the buttons on the radio and stopped at the first few bars of what the announcer later said was a cut from the new Rad McClosky album. She pulled over to the side of the road and parked the car to listen to it. It was a song called "Long Ago Love," backed by bass, piano, and slide guitar, sung in a husky, mournful voice. The guitar was so sharp that Patricia felt her heart was being sliced. Tears came into her eyes. Then she made an illegal U-turn and drove back to the shopping center. At Flame's discount record store she asked the clerk shyly for the new Rad McClosky album, as if it were a phrase in code. She was afraid that she had gotten the name wrong and the clerk would look blankly at her. It was slightly miraculous to her that the clerk nodded and put the record into her hands. On the cover was a picture of Rad McClosky, smiling and scowling —the expression that made him famous. A bright lock of hair fell onto his high forehead.

She drove home impatiently through the traffic, her heart beating with frustration at every red light. She was so eager with her keys that she dropped them at the door. Inside she put the record on and was relieved to find a note from Richard taped to the icebox informing her that he would be home late. It read:

P. Fac. meeting today. Home 6:30 or thereabouts. Fridge filthy, I might add. R.

She listened to both sides of the record twice, sitting on the floor with her ear pressed up against a speaker. She was dazzled and rapt, anxious to memorize all the songs at once. She turned the sound up and went back to the kitchen. The icebox was not filthy that she could see, but dry shreds of lettuce and bread-crumbs littered the bottom. There were faint finger smudges on the door. But if Richard said it was filthy, it probably was. Patricia believed that Richard possessed a higher wisdom, and that her own chief flaw was failure of vision. Richard was very solid: he took responsibility seriously. He took his classes, his marriage, the order of his rooms, and his newspaper in the morning seriously. Richard was the most thoroughly informed person Patricia had ever known. He believed that if you opted, out of conscious will, to do a thing, it should be done completely. In his presence, Patricia knew she was a child. The only thing she knew anything about was music, but this slight knowledge was discounted by Richard on the grounds that she was untrained and couldn't read it. His interest in music was perfunctory. He had a basic record library of the standard obscure classics, and he liked to hear Stravinsky during dinner.

Patricia wished the crumbs in the icebox bothered her; she wished the smudges on the door were offensive. These things ought to matter, she knew, like knowing how to read music if you loved it so. She picked up a rag, intending to clean, but instead she made herself a cup of coffee and listened to Rad McClosky. She realized that she was in the grip of what Richard called "emotional sloppiness," and that it was getting worse. After all, she had *chosen* to stay home and keep house, chosen it over going back to school as Richard suggested. She was not keeping her end of the bargain up. She and Richard had been discussing this of late, and of late Patricia had stopped sleeping properly, stopped cleaning the house properly as she once had, and had stopped reading *Bleak House* two hundred pages in. The application for a modern dance class sat on her bureau, filled out but unsent. It had been there for two months. Sitting over her coffee, Patricia realized that what she *really* wanted to do was to listen to Rad McClosky singing "Closing Doors."

For a month she played the record over and over during the day, and she was afraid that it was getting somewhat worn. There was a small scratch on "Closing Doors" and a larger one on "The Fire in My Heart That Burns for You." She thought she might buy another copy as a contingency, in case the first gave out altogether. At night she suffered slightly that she couldn't listen to it since it disturbed Richard. He was finishing his novel, called *Pain in Its Simplicity,* and he needed quiet. She knew that if she were finishing a novel, she would be annoyed if Richard played Stravinsky all the time and she knew that if that were the case, Richard would be good about Stravinsky. Every night, Richard put in two hours on *Pain in Its Simplicity* and an hour preparing his lectures for the three English courses he taught.

Richard was very sensitive to noise: they had the top floor of an old frame house and Richard had chosen it so there would be no footfall above them. Richard's study faced the yard, but he kept the window closed although no one was ever out back at night. Three walls of solid book shelving kept out even the noise of the wind. While Richard wo:ked on *Pain in Its Simplicity,* Patricia sat in the living room. Through the closed door of the study she could hear the muffled clacking of a typewriter. A copy of *Bleak House* was unopened on her lap: she was reading the back of the Rad McClosky album.

Richard had pursued her: Patricia had been a student in his survey of English Literature 12001. She was a junior in college, and Richard was getting his doctorate. On the first paper she handed in he had written: "This is beneath you. You could do so, so very much better." She realized that special interest was being taken in her, but how did he know that she could do better? When he lectured, he paced, and when he paused to look at her, she was sure she was being seen into. One afternoon he asked her to stay after class: she was certain she was flunking, but he only asked her out to dinner. He began to take her out to dinner once a week, then twice. After a while she discovered that most of her time was spent with him. Her friends, bouncy undergraduates who got together on weekends to dance at the local bar, annoyed him, and gradually she fell away from them. He was interested in seriousness, he said. He was interested in potential. "When I look at you," he would say, "what I see is not some flip kid running around dancing, but a finished person." By spring, Patricia was very strained. She tried spending some time away from Richard, sitting at the bar watching her friends dance. It was what she wanted to do while young. Basically, she was a good-natured girl, known for her high spirits. She wanted to string her college days like bright glass beads, one by one by one. After an evening with her friends, upset at her longing to be what she once was—*just a kid*—she looked in the mirror and realized that what Richard told her must be true: she was past being silly. She was passed being flip. She had to be—there was no future in it. Something about Richard frightened her and she fought against it. One night they discussed it, and Richard told her that she was only frightened of being what she could be, if she wanted to.

"Then what are you hanging around with me for?" Patricia had asked.

"You tell me."

"Because I'm fabulously pretty."

"That's very flip, Pat. As a matter of fact, I don't think you're pretty. From time to time, you're something much better. You're beautiful, but pretty you're not." Then Richard told her that children fooled around, but adults went to bed with each other—which side was she on? She took the side of the adults and it was settled. At the end of her junior year they were married in her parents' house in Connecticut.

In the mornings after Richard left for school, Patricia put on the Rad McClosky record and drank her coffee sitting next to the speaker. She drank two cups of coffee and listened to the record three times. On the shelf above the stereo was a picture of herself and Richard, taken by a friend. They were sitting on a sofa, and Richard's arm was around her. He was medium-sized and wiry, with shiny black hair, straight teeth, and a mustache. Next to him in the photo, she felt she looked flimsy and insubstantial. Her hair curled and fell into her eyes. She was wear-

ing and still wore what Richard called "baby sweaters" and her
legs in their boots twisted around one another. In the photo, he
looked as if he were Architecture, and she was a random, flying
buttress he was supporting.

She was three years married and when she looked at herself in
the mirror, she did not see that she had become any more serious,
any less young and heedless, or any more willing to get down to
what Richard called "the things of life." He was right when he
said that she had not made up her mind about anything. She was
shy in Indiana. There seemed to be a code of life that she didn't
understand. In the East, things had familiar shapes, and a familiar
place to put them in. Born in Connecticut and educated in Cambridge, she felt she was in the midst of an alien order. She felt in
Indiana the way she had felt in France when she was eighteen.
Since Richard was at work on his novel, they kept socializing to a
minimum, except for invitations to dinner parties at faculty
houses, which were repaid by dinner parties at their house. One
afternoon a week she took a bundle of laundry to the laundromat,
and watched a collection of fat women in Hawaiian shirts feeding
towels into the washing machines. In the afternoon she listened to
Rad McClosky and drank coffee. Richard had stopped plaguing
her about *Bleak House* or about the modern dance class. Now he
watched her silently and she felt like a patient about whom the
doctor has said: We can do nothing but wait.

It had been decided, after one long, serious talk, that Patricia
should not do anything until she felt ready, and when she was
ready, she and Richard, together, would work out the details. At
the time she wondered how she would know when she was ready.
Then she had thought that Richard would know.

What she did was listen to Rad McClosky. She learned every
song by heart and knew every nuance. She knew when the guitars
broke in unexpectedly, when the piano took over, and when the
rhythm line changed. While doing the laundry or shopping at the
Great West, she could listen to it in her head, as if there were a
switch in her mind that would play Rad McClosky for her.

Richard's birthday was in April, and three weeks before it Patricia realized that she had no money other than the weekly house money. She knew what she wanted to buy him: a set of the Arden Shakespeare they had seen in a second-hand book store. Richard had always wanted it. While they were still in Cambridge, he used to comparison shop the book stores for a set, but either they were annotated in ballpoint ink, or tattered, or in mint condition and therefore overpriced. In secret, Patricia had gone to the second-hand store, priced it, and calculated how much money she could possibly take out of her house money to add up to forty dollars. But buying Richard a present with house money was wrong: it took food out of his mouth in order to provide him with a gift. Besides, she was buying it with his money. If she asked her parents for a check, it would have to be accounted for.

Finally, she saw a job for a part-time typist advertised and took it. Twice a week for three weeks she sat behind a gray filing cabinet at Harley's Auto Supply and typed out shipping bills. She asked to be paid in cash and hoarded the bills in a spice jar that she hid at the back of a cabinet. It was her constant fear in those three weeks that Richard might decide that the shelves needed rearranging and would come across a jar of coriander with five-dollar bills hidden in it.

Three days before Richard's birthday, Patricia drove to the book store with the jar of coriander in her handbag. At a stoplight on the way it occurred to her that the set might have been sold and she panicked: she had never thought to check if it were still there. Richard was right about her: she simply couldn't plan.

But the set was there—in mint condition—and it was hers for forty dollars. The clerk watched as she produced the jar of coriander and picked the bills out from the seeds.

She took the set home in a carton and hid it under the sink in back of the rags. The day of his birthday, she wrapped each volume in pink and green tissue paper and stacked them back in the carton, which she wrapped in yellow paper and tied with a green bow. In the afternoon she roasted a chicken and made a carrot pudding for Richard's birthday supper. Rad McClosky sang from the living room and she hummed with him. When she looked at the carton sitting on the table, she was dazzled at her accomplishment. With the baster in her hand, she harmonized to "The Fire in My Heart That Burns for You":

"I can't help it, I can't sleep
It's like walking right through smoke
From the fire in my heart that burns for you.
As you sow so shall you reap
But believe me it's no joke
The fire in my heart that burns for you."

Dinner was ready when Richard got home, and the carton was sitting on his chair. He pulled his chair out, saw it, and asked Patricia what it was.

"It's your birthday present," she said. Richard looked at it with suspicion, but he was visibly touched.

"Should I open it now or wait till after dinner?" he asked.

"After," said Patricia, but it was a bad choice. She could scarcely eat in anticipation.

Dinner finished, Richard untied the green ribbon and tore off the yellow paper. Then he took the tissue paper carefully from each volume and stacked them on the table. He pushed his chair back and asked Patricia where she got the money to buy it.

"I worked as a typist, part-time."

"Where?"

"At a place called Harley's Auto Supply off Route 3."

"Why did you do that?"

She looked at him, on the verge of tears. "To get your birthday present for you."

Richard drummed his fingers on the top volume. Then he folded the tissue paper neatly and restacked the books in the carton. Patricia watched him, squinting, one leg wrapped around the other.

"I'm very touched," said Richard. "But we have to take them back."

"But you said . . . when we were downtown, you always said you wanted it."

"Pat, I'm very touched, but I think you misunderstand. I'm really touched that you wanted to get me a birthday present, but I can't possibly approve of what you did to get it. If you wanted to work, you should work for *you,* not to get things for me. It's a way of buying me. I couldn't possibly keep this knowing that you worked at some awful job to get it for me. It's slavish."

By this time, Patricia was weeping into her napkin. "I don't think they'll take it back," she said. "It's second-hand."

"I want you to do things for you, Pat," said Richard softly.

The following Saturday, they drove downtown. The bookstore would not take back the set of the Arden Shakespeare since it was second-hand, although in mint condition. Richard was silent on the drive back, and Patricia thought he was angry, but at home he arranged the set carefully on one of his shelves. He displaced several volumes of Matthew Arnold, George Meredith, and Henry James in the process. He spent the rest of the afternoon rearranging his shelves in order to find a proper slot for each one.

Monday afternoon, Richard came home early. Patricia was sitting in front of the speaker listening to Rad McClosky. She had hardly moved out of the chair all day. She heard the key turn in the door and Richard appeared.

"Hello," she said brightly.

"Would you turn that off, please?"

Patricia switched off the stereo and sat back in her chair.

"Pat," said Richard. "What's wrong?"

"Nothing's wrong. I'm just fine."

"Pat, you are *not* just fine. You haven't been fine for quite a while. I've been very concerned about you recently, and we haven't talked about it at all. I came home early today to really sit down with you."

"There's nothing wrong," said Patricia. "I'm fine."

"Pat, come on. You've let everything go. You don't seem to want to do anything any more. You fall into this childish ennui. There are any number of things you can do, you know that. But it seems to me that all you do is sit around the house and listen to that ape boy and his slide guitars. Is that what you do?"

Patricia stood up and took the record off the record player. Then she broke it over her knee.

"No," she said.

That night she slept badly. There had been no fight, no discussion. At dinner, Richard began to speak of her inability to cope, a favorite phrase of his, and Patricia uttered six commonplace words she had never said before as a sentence. "I don't want to discuss it," she said. After dinner Richard worked on *Pain in Its Simplicity* and his lectures. Patricia hemmed a skirt and was in bed with the light off when Richard came to sleep. He went to sleep at once: he was an immediate but light sleeper. Patricia was stiff on her side of the bed. She knew how easily his sleep was broken and she didn't want to interrupt it. Tears spilled out of her eyes and down her cheeks. She wondered if she had broken the record out of childish pique or as a concession to Richard, a sign that she would do better. Then she wondered how she was going to live without Rad McClosky, and the tears spilled faster. She looked over at Richard, asleep on his side in striped pajamas. They were as separate as the eggs in the icebox. After lying awake rigidly for hours, she fell asleep as the dawn came up. When she woke it was ten thirty and Richard had gone to his classes.

She made the bed, had a cup of coffee, and washed the dishes. In the living room she saw that the record was lying on the floor in two jagged pieces. Richard had left them there to remind her. She picked them up and tried to fit the pieces together. They connected for an instant and fell apart in her hands. She threw them into the wicker basket. Then she sat in the chair in front of the stereo and thought about her first college beau, and of her roommate. She was the same girl now that she had been then, she thought. She went into the bedroom and packed a book bag with two pairs of underpants, a blouse and skirt, a comb, brush, and extra toothbrush—nothing that would be missed. She wrote a note and taped it to the icebox, the place messages were left. It read:

> Richard: The car is in my name and I am taking it for a drive. I may be back, but may not. Patricia.

She drove to Flame's Discount Record store and bought another copy of *Closing Doors*. Once in the car, she was confronted with Indiana. All she knew of it was the triangle that formed her life there: from house to downtown, from downtown to University, and from University to shopping center. Even Harley's Auto Supply had fallen within this pattern. The thought of the expressway frightened her: sign upon sign upon sign. Besides, it was a toll road and she had only six dollars, Rad McClosky having claimed four of her ten. She drove away from Flame's on a road she had never taken. She knew it did not lead downtown, or to the University, or to home. For an hour she drove abstractly with the radio on, past rows of frame houses, past factories and oil refineries. She passed through a series of small towns. At the edge of each was a marker giving its name, date of founding, and density of population. She was welcomed by the Elks, Optimists, Kiwanis, and Hoosier clubs, and the Methodist and Episcopal churches. After three hours, she knew she was lost. Listening to the radio distracted her and she had made several turns. She thought she might drive to Connecticut, but she had no idea what highway to take, how long the trip would be, how much the tolls and gas would cost. Besides, if she got to Connecticut, what would she say? She was not a daughter: she was a wife.

The radio played all the songs she liked, "Closing Doors," "Hickory Holler's Tramp," and "A Road in Arkansas." She sang the chorus:

"Down this road in Arkansas, I can't even see a sign
My tears have lead me down the highway

All I know is you're not mine, and I'm lonely and I'm poor
And I'm stranded on this road in Arkansas."

She tried to substitute "Indiana" for "Arkansas" but it didn't fit.

       She wondered what Richard was doing, if he had
come home early and found her note. Would he call the highway
patrol, or would he wait for her to come back? If she called the
house, would he be there? It would be easy enough to get back: all
she need do was pull in at a gas station and get directions.

She was in the middle of a flat road, surrounded by mud-colored fields. If she got home before Richard, she could untape the
note and he would never know that she had left. If she came back
and he was there, he would be sitting in the study or in the living
room with her note in his hand. It got later as she drove.

A light rain smudged the windshield. The sky darkened and
large drops hit the windows on a slant. The road was shiny and
slick.

"The next gas station," she said aloud. "I'll stop at the next gas
station."

The sky was the color of tin. She looked at her watch and it
was much later in the afternoon than she had thought. A sign on
the road said "Gas five miles." She drove until she could see a
Gulf sign around the bend. She stayed on the right, and signaled
to turn, but her hand stayed steady on the wheel and she looked at
the road ahead through the spaces the windshield wipers cleared
for her. Finally, she saw the Gulf station in the rear-view mirror.

She made a pact that she would stop at the next one. She swore
she would. She was longing to turn back. Miles of gray road
stretched in front of her. Her foot was tired on the accelerator. On
the seat next to her was the new copy of *Closing Doors*. When she
saw the sign announcing gas in three miles, she was filled with
gladness and resolve. Coming up to it she could see that it was a
brick station with a shingled roof. She downshifted carefully into
third. It was Richard who had taught her how to drive a stick
shift. He had been very patient. "It's the only way to drive, Pat. If

you're going to drive a car, you may as well drive a real one," he had said.

Her blinker signaled a right turn. There were no cars in back of her. Her hand went out and she turned on the radio up full, so loud that she could not hear the rain. Shifting into fourth she shot past the station and looked into the rear-view mirror only when she knew it would be a dot far off down the road.

 # the smartest woman
in america

Essie beck is sitting in a hotel room in Washington, D.C. The television is on with the sound turned down, for she feels quite close to the pulse of the news. Her hotel room is a comfortable one—it has none of the cheap, rough edges of hotel rooms—pale, soft, and expensive, and Essie is sitting in one of its soft, old-world chairs. Her feet, in flannel travel slippers, are resting on a table. With one hand she is making corrections on her lecture with a ballpoint pen. There are very few corrections to be made in this paper—she has been over it five times and is completely satisfied with it, although by this time it has the stale quality of home-baked pastry overadmired by its cook.

The mouths of the newsmen flap open and shut and they might be singing opera for all the interest she has in them. They have already reported that the Smartest Woman in America Competition is in its final stages and that tomorrow the contestants are to tape their lectures. Tomorrow, at 10:45, Essie will go to the Educational Television studio, where she will read her paper and be taped. This is the final leg of the competition, which she knows with a feeling of certainty, warm as the inside of a piece of toast, she will win. The only hook into her sureness is that she does not know who the other contestants are. It is a rule of the contest that the participants are not publicly announced, never see or confront one another, and in fact never know who the other contestants are until after the winner has been selected.

Another of the provisions is that during the final judging (which is done by televising the taped lectures to a panel of judges in the studio), the contestants must be on their various ways home, so that even then they cannot see themselves or their rivals. Several months ago, when the rules were sent to Essie, she expressed puzzlement.

"I don't really understand that," Essie said to her husband, Stuart.

"It gives it a certain purity," said Stuart. "I mean, what did you expect, Es? To get orchids for being the smartest woman in America? This isn't a quiz show, with prizes. It puts the competitive element on a higher plane."

"I still think it's kind of odd," Essie said.

"Intelligence," said Stuart, pulling on his pipe, "is its own reward."

It is a very dignified contest judged by two college presidents, the Secretary of Health, Education and Welfare, the head of the National Science Foundation, the education editor of *The New York Times,* a senior editor from a distinguished publishing house, and the head of the Ford Foundation. The five finalists are given a loose topic, made up by the panel of judges, and each composes a paper. This year's topic is "The Effect of Technology on the Human Spirit." Essie, who teaches contemporary literature, has written on "Pollution and the Human Spirit in Contemporary American Fiction." It is a splendid and capable paper. It is not out of any intellectual aggression that she knows she will win: she simply knows a good thing when she sees it.

Small, runty, and rooty, she looks like a young edition of an old, gnarled tree. She has wispy brown hair, cut short and efficient. Both she and Stuart, a lawyer, have sober, unimaginative faces. In this serious world they are not often amused, but an occasional cartoon in *The New Yorker* makes them laugh politely. The two of them hang together like icicles. They have never been asked, but if they were, they would say that love is not an issue relevant to the twentieth century. They will eventually have two children. Life is tidy and satisfactory and functional, like water— good in itself. Although they are healthy in the way wiry people are, they often look a bit seedy, as if they suffered from minor ailments such as falling arches and thinning hair. But they suffer from neither: they merely look as if they do.

Two nights ago, Essie and Stuart were sitting over coffee on Riverside Drive. The Sharps and the Robarts had been over for dinner and Alice Robart had done the dishes "to take some of the strain off," though Essie insisted that the strain wasn't on. Then they left, and Essie and Stuart were talking about what the ghost of Hamlet's father means.

"I think it's just to bring the familial element into very strong focus," Essie said.

"Well, it could be a kind of legal device. It lets the audience know that a wrong has been done and that Hamlet is in the right," said Stuart. Whenever they discussed anything, they sat very eagerly, their upper torsos pressing against the table.

"But it also has to do with Hamlet's madness," Essie said.

"Yes, dear. But in Shakespeare's time, they did believe in ghosts, so Hamlet's madness has nothing to do with that. It's on another level entirely."

Essie bit at her cuticle. She is a reasonable woman. There was something to that.

Later, she sat in bed rereading *The Scarlet Letter*. Stuart sat on his side of the bed in striped pajamas, reading *Foreign Affairs*. He smelled of fresh towels.

"Say, Es. You're only in Washington for two days, you ought to splurge. Buy a dress where all the Senate wives get theirs."

"It's no big event," said Essie, but it wasn't a bad idea.

"Will you get your hair done?" he asked, loading his pipe. He always had a pipe before bed.

"Hair done? Good Lord, no. I haven't had my hair done in years, since college graduation."

"You had your hair done when we got married," said Stuart, puffing.

"That was different."

"Well, but you'll be on television."

"That," said Essie, "is their business, not mine. Besides, why should I have my brain fried by a hair dryer. I couldn't possibly read under one of those things, with all those chattering women. As you said, this is a dignified event, not a quiz show. I'm supposed to look like a college professor, which is what I am."

"You could have it done dignified," Stuart suggested.

"Stuart," said Essie, in the clipped twang she saved for being annoyed, "hairdressers can't be trusted. I see no reason why I should look like Lady Astor's horse just to read a paper on pollution and literature on television."

"It's national . . ."

"I'm fine just the way I am. I'll just be who I am," said Essie.

"It's just a thought, Es. It'll be like a little vacation for you."

"It'll be just like being here, except I'll be in Washington."

"Just a thought," he said, knocking out his pipe.

The lights hang around like gnats, but gnats made out of neon or tiny two-hundred-watt bulbs. They seem to be pointed at her eyes, and she blinks behind the glasses she wears for reading and going to the movies. "Too much light off those glasses," says a young man in a blue shirt, consulting his light meter. Next to him is a mustachioed man with a camera who is taking still shots for the newspaper.

"Have her sit down, like she's reading her lecture," he says.

"Really, I think this is silly," says Essie. An older man appears. He looks rather like the man who had been her dissertation adviser.

"Can you get her to sit and pose reading her lecture?" the man with the camera asks him.

"Mrs. Beck, I'm the director of this show. Can you sit and look as if you're reading your lecture, so the newspapers can have a picture?"

"I think it's really very silly," says Essie.

"For the newspapers, Mrs. Beck." He takes her elbow, as if she were a mental patient. "Can you put your head up, Mrs. Beck?" says the man with the camera.

"How can I read with my head up?" she asks, sharply.

"We won't be able to see your face. Anyway, you're not supposed to *read*. You're only supposed to look like it." She looks up, but just. The man with the camera shoots. Little points of light concentrate in the middle of her eyes. Squinting, she takes a hard look at the director, wondering how she can get him to tell her who the competition is. Since he looks like her dissertation adviser, she decides he is the one to approach. She is thinking of a subtle way to ask, but the director interrupts.

"Now, Mrs. Beck," he says. "I'll take you to the set. We had it decorated like a home library. It's very tasteful. Underdone. You'll be very comfortable." He takes her by the elbow and leads her deeper into the studio, stepping over pythonlike cables and wormy strings of wires. Alone and abandoned amidst huge cameras, spotlights hanging like iron bananas, machines on dollies, drooping microphones and more wires is the "set," a room with two of its walls hacked off, lined with bookshelves. The books are old leatherbound law reviews, *The Congressional Record, Diseases of the Skin,* Volumes VI through XLV, and an encyclopedia. There is also a desk with false drawers on the front and no back. She sits in the chair provided for her and looks out over the desk.

Several men appear, armed with light meters, cables, and sound boxes. Three more ride on huge moving cameras that poke their snouts at and away from her. Over her head, a man is sitting on a metal catwalk surrounded by sound equipment. The director hangs a wire around her neck. At the end of it is a little metal pencil that he tells her is the microphone. "Talk into it," he says.

"Hello . . . hello," says Essie.

"Is that coming up, Jimmy?" he yells.

"She has to say more," answers a disembodied voice.

"You have to say more," the director says.

"My topic is pollution and the human spirit in contemporary

American fiction," says Essie into the microphone.

"Not so close into the mike," shouts Jimmy.

"You have to speak above it, Mrs. Beck. Not into it."

"My topic is pollution and the human spirit in contemporary American fiction," she says carefully above her metal pencil.

"O.K.," says Jimmy.

"Now Mrs. Beck," says the director, "we've timed your speech . . ."

She interrupts. "It's not a speech. It's a paper."

"Your paper," says the director. "We read it through, and it should take twenty minutes, give or take. Now the thing to remember is: don't rush, and just speak as you would normally." He emphasizes the word "normally." "I think you should read us several paragraphs just so we'll get the feel of your voice."

Essie Beck gives him a professorial, puzzled look. The *feel* of her voice? As she begins to read, another man appears, carrying a doctor's satchel.

"Excuse me, Mrs. Beck. This is our makeup man. Put the lights full, Charlie." The lights go up. Essie Beck squints.

"Not so full on the eyes," says the director, checking out her glasses. The lights dim.

"I think," the makeup man says, "we need a little powder. Just around the eyes and nose. And a little eye liner."

"Wait a minute," says Essie. "Am I supposed to read a few paragraphs or not?"

"In a minute, Mrs. Beck. Just a little powder," says the director.

"This is not a quiz show. I'm a college professor, not a model."

"Certainly, Mrs. Beck," says the director, looking at her. "This is a very dignified competition, but it's still television."

"If you don't have some powder, you'll come out like a shiny pumpkin," adds the makeup man.

Essie Beck looks at him. "Oh, will I," she says tartly.

"It's just a little," explains the makeup man. "We have to do it —the lights and all. Really, everyone has to have it. Walter

Cronkite has it. Even the President has it. All the other ladies we taped had it."

"All right," says Essie. "But just a little." She suffers her face to be powdered. A slimy feeling runs across her eyelids as the eye liner is applied.

"O.K.," says the makeup man grimly, stepping back. "Great."

While they set the lights and position the camera, Essie wonders who "all the other ladies" are. She and Stuart have made calculated guesses: after all, the community of scholars is small and interwoven. They are pretty sure that one is Joan Splenny, the constitutional law scholar, and another is probably Sylvia Vesparrugio, the marine biologist. One of them, she is very sure, is Virginia Cadwalder, her old Radcliffe rival, a sociologist. According to the alumnae bulletin, Virginia Cadwalder appeared in the "People Are Talking About" section of *Vogue*, and it is Essie's belief that she is not a reliable academic.

"Tell me," says Essie to the director in a carefully absent tone, "have you taped Virginia Cadwalder yet?"

"Now Mrs. Beck, you know it's against the rules and spirit of this competition to say who's in it."

"I'd forgotten," she says in her Oxford ladies' college voice. She settles in her chair as they adjust the lights for the last time. The powder weighs heavily on her face and she feels somewhat smudgy about the eyes, but still, she is beyond confidence. Under the desk she crosses her feet and lets her heels slip out of her shoes. Now she feels just as if she were on Riverside Drive with her bedroom slippers on.

She arranges her notes in front of her and gives the first page a brief, satisfied skim-through. They are all lined up in front of her: the director, the makeup man, the gaffers, and the camera grips, the sound men, and the newspaper photographers. The cameras move in like tanks. They are taking her in. The makeup man whispers "hair" to the director, who looks at her and shakes his head. She feels as Moses must have felt confronting a line of Israelites before giving them the Ten Commandments.

As a last touch, one of them puts a little plastic sign in front of her. It reads, in raised black letters on a gray background: *Essa-line T. Beck.*

"My topic is pollution and the human spirit in contemporary American fiction," she begins.

Stuart Beck fills his pipe. He has had dinner out and is drinking a cup of Sanka. The television is on and the announcer is talking about the Smartest Woman in America Competition, what it means to education and to women in general. Then the judges are presented. They appear in various states of tweed and pin stripe, looking either as bland as squash or pinched and harried. The famous editor looks like a boyish gangster. The President has sent his good wishes and his hopes that events of this sort will set an example for the youth of the nation. A lady journalist makes a short speech. She says that although the winner will not, of course, *be* the smartest woman in America, she will be a symbol of all that is best in women, and that this competition gives stature to the cause of women's rights and is an inspiration to young girls. Now the papers are to be read. The first is given by Sylvia Vesparrugio, the marine biologist. Stuart drowses over *The New Statesman,* pleased that he and Essie have guessed one right.

"I only half watched, Es. Yours was clearly the only relevant one," he will say.

Next comes an ecologist whose name is unfamiliar to Stuart. He writes it down on a pad. Then Joan Splenny, the constitutional law scholar, appears, and Stuart smiles to himself. Finally there is Essie, and there will be one more after her. The commentator says her name, where she went to school, where she got each of her three degrees, in what journals she has published, and that her husband is Stuart Beck, a New York lawyer who with his wife is co-author of a monograph entitled *Law in the Novels of Charles Dickens.*

Essie's face is on the screen, blurred by the lines of the television. Stuart wonders if a face he knows so well is blurred, how blurred are the faces he doesn't know? He makes a note on the pad to call the television repair people. Her face is flat, like a face on a poster. Stuart fiddles with the fine tuner, trying to get a clearer picture, but it remains fuzzy. Essie reads her paper, looking up from time to time, glittering behind her spectacles. It is clearly the best speech. Stuart wonders who the last contestant will be. He hopes it will be Virginia Cadwalder: Essie will be so glad to beat her. He could recite the paper along with Essie, they have been over it so many times. When she is finished, she smiles the smile of a lecturer and is followed by the announcement of a future program about Uganda.

Essie is being lifted away from Washington, and the lights on the runway blink spastically. She has rather liked Washington. A member of the National Science Foundation took her to the National Gallery. She sits back in her seat, comfortable in the knowledge that Stuart is at home on Riverside Drive watching her on television. She has never been in two places at the same time before. At this moment, the thing she wants most is to see the pad on which Stuart has promised to write the names of the other contestants. It is the horsefly in the ointment of her satisfaction that she doesn't know whom she is beating. Since it is obvious to her that she will win, it not a question of tension or nerves, but she wants to know what she calls "the level of the competition." After the taping she was shown around the studio, feigning interest, but what she was really after was any chart, program sheet, schedule, or announcement that would tell her what she wanted to know. When she left the studio she looked at the doorman and wondered if *he* knew and were approachable. The thought occurred to her in a weak moment that money buys information, but she rejected it immediately as a notion born of the corrupting influence of having been in a television studio.

On the plane she almost itches with irritation that she cannot even *see* who the contestants are. It is a short flight from Washington to New York, and a short ride from the airport to Riverside Drive. Stuart offered to pick her up, but his place is by the television set, marking down the names of the other women. Of course, in a few hours she will know who they are, but she will not be able to witness their performance until the award ceremony at the Smithsonian, when the entire program will be rebroadcast. Then she will get her award—a money grant—which she will use to finish her book on linguistics and the ethics of American fiction.

She is quite comfortable, and it is not until midway through the flight that an image of Virginia Cadwalder flashes through her mind, sporting a halo on which the words "People Are Talking About" are printed. She wishes that she believed in telepathic communication and that she were in communication with Stuart right now. Then she pushes Virginia Cadwalder out of her mind and begins to make mental notes of her acceptance speech. Finally, she projects the smile of triumph on Stuart's face when she walks in the door.

The stewardess brings her a snack of Danish and coffee, which she exchanges for Sanka. She feels somewhat cheated that the stewardess does not know who she is and what she has done. It would have been nice to be recognized. But of course tomorrow they will all know not only who she is and what she has done, but *what* she is: the Smartest Woman in America.

The man sitting next to her is sleeping with his mouth open and as he sighs, a little puff of gin emerges. Finally he wakes up and stretches. Of course he has no way of knowing who is sitting next to him. He pulls *The New York Times* out of his briefcase and starts to work on the half-finished crossword puzzle, but he is stuck on a French composer, five letters long, whose third letter is "t."

Essie reads over his shoulder. "Satie," she says. It fits. He thanks her.

mr. parker

Mrs. Parker died suddenly in October. She and Mr. Parker lived in a Victorian house next to ours, and Mr. Parker was my piano teacher. He commuted to Wall Street, where he was a securities analyst, but he had studied at Juilliard and gave lessons on the side—for the pleasure of it, not for money. His only students were me and the church organist, who was learning technique on a double-keyboard harpsichord Mr. Parker had built one spring.

Mrs. Parker was known for her pastry; she and my mother were friends, after a fashion. Every two months or so they spent a day together in the kitchen baking butter cookies and cream puffs, or rolling out strudel leaves. She was thin and wispy, and turned out her pastry with abstract expertness. As a girl, she had had bright-red hair, which was now the color of old leaves. There was something smoky and autumnal about her: she wore rust-colored sweaters and heather-colored skirts, and kept dried weeds in ornamental jars and pressed flowers in frames. If you borrowed a book from her, there were petal marks on the back pages. She was tall, but she stooped as if she had spent a lifetime looking for something she had dropped.

The word "tragic" was mentioned in connection with her death. She and Mr. Parker were in the middle of their middle age, and

127

neither of them had ever been seriously ill. It was heart failure, and unexpected. My parents went to see Mr. Parker as soon as they got the news, since they took their responsibilities as neighbors seriously, and two days later they took me to pay a formal condolence call. It was Indian summer, and the house felt closed in. They had used the fireplace during a recent cold spell, and the living room smelled faintly of ash. The only people from the community were some neighbors, the minister and his wife, and the rabbi and his wife and son. The Parkers were Episcopalian, but Mr. Parker played the organ in the synagogue on Saturday mornings and on High Holy Days. There was a large urn of tea, and the last of Mrs. Parker's strudel. On the sofa were Mrs. Parker's sisters, and a man who looked like Mr. Parker ten years younger leaned against the piano, which was closed. The conversation was hushed and stilted. On the way out, the rabbi's son tried to trip me, and I kicked him in return. We were adolescent enemies of a loving sort, and since we didn't know what else to do, we expressed our love in slaps and pinches and other mild attempts at grievous bodily harm.

I loved the Parkers' house. It was the last Victorian house on the block, and was shaped like a wedding cake. The living room was round, and all the walls curved. The third floor was a tower, on top of which sat a weathervane. Every five years the house was painted chocolate brown, which faded gradually to the color of weak tea. The front-hall window was a stained-glass picture of a fat Victorian baby holding a bunch of roses. The baby's face was puffy and neuter, and its eyes were that of an old man caught in a state of surprise. Its white dress was milky when the light shone through.

On Wednesday afternoons, Mr. Parker came home on an early train, and I had my lesson. Mr. Parker's teaching method never varied. He never scolded or corrected. The first fifteen minutes were devoted to a warmup in which I could play anything I liked. Then Mr. Parker played the lesson of the week. His playing was terrifically precise, but his eyes became dreamy and unfocused. Then

I played the same lesson, and after that we worked on the difficult passages, but basically he wanted me to hear my mistakes. When we began a new piece, we played it part by part, taking turns, over and over.

After that, we sat in the solarium and discussed the next week's lesson. Mr. Parker usually played a record and talked in detail about the composer, his life and times, and the form. With the exception of Mozart and Schubert, he liked Baroque music almost exclusively. The lesson of the week was always Bach, which Mr. Parker felt taught elegance and precision. Mrs. Parker used to leave us a tray of cookies and lemonade, cold in the summer and hot in the winter, with cinnamon sticks. When the cookies were gone, the lesson was over and I left, passing the Victorian child in the hallway.

In the days after the funeral, my mother took several casseroles over to Mr. Parker and invited him to dinner a number of times. For several weeks he revolved between us, the minister, and the rabbi. Since neither of my parents cared much about music, except to hear my playing praised, the conversation at dinner was limited to the stock market and the blessings of country life.

In a few weeks, I got a note from Mr. Parker enclosed in a thank-you note to my parents. It said that piano lessons would begin the following Wednesday.

I went to the Parkers' after school. Everything was the same. I warmed up for fifteen minutes, Mr. Parker played the lesson, and I repeated it. In the solarium were the usual cookies and lemonade.

"Are they good, these cookies?" Mr. Parker asked.

I said they were.

"I made them yesterday," he said. "I've got to be my own baker now."

Mr. Parker's hair had once been blond, but was graying into the color of straw. Both he and Mrs. Parker seemed to have faded out of some bright time they once had lived in. He was very thin, as if the friction of living had burned every unnecessary particle off him, but he was calm and cheery in the way you expect plump people to be. On teaching days, he always wore a blue cardigan, buttoned, and a striped tie. Both smelled faintly of tobacco. At the end of the lesson, he gave me a robin's egg he had found. The light was flickering through the bunch of roses in the window as I left.

When I got home, I found my mother in the kitchen, waiting and angry.

"Where were you?" she said.

"At my piano lesson."

"What piano lesson?"

"You know what piano lesson. At Mr. Parker's."

"You didn't tell me you were going to a piano lesson," she said.

"I always have a lesson on Wednesday."

"I don't want you having lessons there now that Mrs. Parker's gone." She slung a roast into a pan.

I stomped off to my room and wrapped the robin's egg in a sweat sock. My throat felt shriveled and hot.

At dinner, my mother said to my father, "I don't want Jane taking piano lessons from Mr. Parker now that Mrs. Parker's gone."

"Why don't you want me to have lessons?" I said, close to shouting. "There's no reason."

"She can study with Mrs. Murchison." Mrs. Murchison had been my first teacher. She was a fat, myopic woman who smelled of bacon grease and whose repertoire was confined to "Little Classics for Children." Her students were mostly under ten, and she kept an asthmatic chow who was often sick on the rug.

"I won't go to Mrs. Murchison!" I shouted. "I've outgrown her."

"Let's be sensible about this," said my father. "Calm down, Janie."

I stuck my fork into a potato to keep from crying and muttered melodramatically that I would hang myself before I'd go back to Mrs. Murchison.

The lessons continued. At night I practiced quietly, and from time to time my mother would look up and say, "That's nice, dear." Mr. Parker had given me a Three-Part Invention, and I worked on it as if it were granite. It was the most complicated piece of music I had ever played, and I learned it with a sense of loss; since I didn't know when the ax would fall, I thought it might be the last piece of music I would ever learn from Mr. Parker.

The lessons went on and nothing was said, but when I came home after them my mother and I faced each other with division and coldness. Mr. Parker bought a kitten called Mildred to keep him company in the house. When we had our cookies and lemonade, Mildred got a saucer of milk.

At night, I was grilled by my mother as we washed the dishes. I found her sudden interest in the events of my day unnerving. She was systematic, beginning with my morning classes, ending in the afternoon. In the light of her intense focus, everything seemed wrong. Then she said, with arch sweetness, "And how is Mr. Parker, dear?"

"Fine."

"And how are the lessons going?"

"Fine."

"And how is the house now that Mrs. Parker's gone?"

"It's the same. Mr. Parker bought a kitten." As I said it, I knew it was betrayal.

"What kind of kitten?"

"A sort of pink one."

"What's its name?"

"It doesn't have one," I said.

One night she said, "Does Mr. Parker drink?"

"He drinks lemonade."

"I only asked because it must be so hard for him," she said in an offended voice. "He must be very sad."

"He doesn't seem all that sad to me." It was the wrong thing to say.

"I see," she said, folding the dish towel with elaborate care. "You know how I feel about this, Jane. I don't want you alone in the house with him."

"He's my *piano* teacher." I was suddenly in tears, so I ran out of the kitchen and up to my room.

She followed me up, and sat on the edge of my bed while I sat at the desk, secretly crying onto the blotter.

"I only want what's best for you," she said.

"If you want what's best for me, why don't you want me to have piano lessons?"

"I *do* want you to have piano lessons, but you're growing up and it doesn't look right for you to be in a house alone with a widowed man."

"I think you're crazy."

"I don't think you understand what I'm trying to say. You're not a little girl any more, Jane. There are privileges of childhood, and privileges of adulthood, and you're in the middle. It's difficult, I know."

"You don't know. You're just trying to stop me from taking piano lessons."

She stood up. "I'm trying to protect you," she said. "What if Mr. Parker touched you? What would you do then?" She made the word "touch" sound sinister.

"You're just being mean," I said, and by this time I was crying openly. It would have fixed things to throw my arms around her, but that meant losing, and this was war.

"We'll discuss it some other time," she said, close to tears herself.

I worked on the Invention until my hands shook. When I came home, if the house was empty, I practiced in a panic, and finally, it was almost right. On Wednesday, I went to Mr. Parker's and stood at the doorway, expecting something drastic and changed, but it was all the same. There were cookies and lemonade in the solarium. Mildred took a nap on my coat. My fifteen-minute warmup was terrible; I made mistakes in the simplest parts, in things I knew by heart. Then Mr. Parker played the lesson of the week and I tried to memorize his phrasing exactly. Before my turn came, Mr. Parker put the metronome on the floor and we watched Mildred trying to catch the arm.

I played it, and I knew it was right—I was playing music, not struggling with a lesson.

When I was finished, Mr. Parker grabbed me by the shoulders. "That's perfect! Really perfect!" he said. "A real breakthrough. These are the times that make teachers glad they teach."

We had lemonade and cookies and listened to some Palestrina motets. When I left, it was overcast, and the light was murky and green.

I walked home slowly, divided by dread and joy in equal parts. I had performed like an adult, and had been congratulated by an adult, but something had been closed off. I sat under a tree and cried like a baby. He had touched me after all.

imelda

SHE CALLED HERSELF Imelda and she said she
was a cook. Since her English was scanty, she was restricted to
words of one syllable: "yes," "no," and "what," with the exception
of "O.K." and "chicken," which she pronounced "chicking." The
family spoke several phrases in Spanish, but hers was an idiomatic
Colombian, and since in mid-conversation she often dissolved
into fits of giggling, even well-known phrases were generally in-
decipherable.

The family were the Jacobys: father Irwin, mother Grace, son
Fritz, and daughter Jane Catherine. They lived in a large apartment overlooking the Metropolitan Museum of Art, in the
Chinese collection of which Jane Catherine had arranged her
prepubescent assignations behind the ornamental urns. The Jacobys were victims of the servant problem: Suzie, their agèd cook,
had died on them and had been followed by a series of noncook-
ing domestics whose common problem was weak feet. Imelda was
sent to them by an agency, and they hired her out of desperation,
but Grace Jacoby thought it would be useful as well as educational to have some Spanish spoken in the house. Imelda cooked
like a dream, and so, despite the fact that she rarely spoke and
when she did could not be understood, everyone was satisfied.
Her only drawbacks were the giggle, which Jane Catherine called

"a crystal smasher," and an unnervingly placid smile.

Imelda was not her real name: it was later discovered by Jane Catherine that "Imelda" was the name of a song that had been number one on the Bogotá hit parade for a year. Imelda's real name was Zaida Escribano, and the label that issued "Imelda" was Zaida Records Company. This information was revealed to Jane Catherine one afternoon when she found a copy of "Imelda" stuck in between two vintage Ricardo Ray singles at a record store called Discos Latinos. She found this information compelling, but the family was unmoved by it.

Jane Catherine, the family daughter, was problematic. She had long chestnut-colored hair, eyes the color of túrtle shells, and she was fresh.

"This fresh mouth of yours does not endear you to me," Grace Jacoby said to her daughter.

"You have to love me. I'm your child."

"I was speaking of charm, not love."

"Love's more important," Jane Catherine said, "so I'm not terribly worried."

Most difficult to contend with was that Jane Catherine could not be threatened. She had been born smart, which was bad enough, but worse, she seemed to have been born wise. Jane Catherine was unflappable. She was effortless and constantly threw back at her parents examples from the sense of values they had taught her, by which she knew that love was better than charm. Since she knew that she was lovable, she did not go much out of her way to be affable. Most of her spare time was spent hanging around Discos Latinos or at the Bronx Music Palace in the company of her loved one, Tito Ricardo-Ruiz, who, fortunately for Grace Jacoby's peace of mind, was an upper-class Argentinian whose father was with the embassy.

Tito had a true slum streak for which Jane Catherine revered him. She could not get over his penchant for the cheap and the magnificent. In his room, concealed from the Olympian eyes of his parents, were his American treasures: an enormous plaster saint in orange and blue, wearing a purple robe; a candle in the shape of the Empire State Building; a cigarette lighter in the shape of a motorcycle, and four crates full of records. His most treasured item of clothing was a sleazy yellow-and-green jacket made of artificial silk with "Perflex Valve Company" embroidered on the back. He was the darling of the embassy, but he hung around Suggie's, a place noted for mediocre pizza and a terrific jukebox with the same sleepy casualness. His smile, which was slow, was also spectacular, and it rendered him virtually untouchable. His manners, when he needed them, were almost otherworldly, and in adult company he glowed like a slightly fallen angel.

Jane Catherine had been drawn to him at a party given by the Bieberman twins, Libby and Brenda. Their father was a millionaire. Jane Catherine, whose few feelings about the twins included contempt and scorn, watched her peer group play under a number of large Renoirs. Tito's parents' house was filled with pre-Columbian statuary in glass cases, so he was unimpressed. Jane Catherine was wise enough to know that everyone had Renoirs: her family had a school of Raphael drawing, several small Matisses, and some Albert Pinkham Ryder. The Jacobys knew what *they* were about.

The music provided by the Bieberman twins was loud, and in the opinion of Jane Catherine, undanceable, until, by accident, someone put on a samba record, at which point Tito and Jane Catherine found each other and danced. It was for this moment that Jane Catherine had practiced in the mirror, had put up with her Uncle Seymour's cha-cha, and her father's ritual New Year's Eve party rhumba. After a trip to Rio, Mrs. Jacoby taught her the bossa nova, and the samba came to her naturally. The only thing Fritz had ever taught her was how to steal records. Hence the consummate product Tito held in his arms, dancing to Jackie Cruz and his Latin Rhythm Kings.

Tito, it was clear, was not in the same league as the bland, clammy group of prep-school boys the Biebermans and their friends found enthralling. It was for him that diplomatic immunity had been invented. Had it not been for the special tags on his license plate, he would have been good for about eight years in jail, in speeding violations alone. His glove compartment was filled with tickets, which he dumped every couple of months into the incinerator off the pantry. He had just turned seventeen, but already he had been propositioned by several of his mother's friends and had ridden a horse in a race in Buenos Aires. The fathers of his classmates were aware of his large store of Cuban cigars, and were often put in the humiliating position of cadging. For this reason, Tito kept several in his jacket on all social occasions.

Tito's brother was at Harvard, and Fritz was away at school, and since the Jacobys and the Ricardos were frequently out, Tito and Jane Catherine found considerable time to be alone. Imelda was invisible and the Ricardo servants, whom Tito called "the Incas of Eighty-third Street," were virtually deaf and perpetually mute, so Tito and Jane Catherine spent many happy hours engaged in adolescent love. If the Jacobys and the Ricardos were in, they went sulkily to the movies, or to Suggie's. They did not much fraternize with their peers, whom they found trying and silly. Since Tito's father kept a horse—a fact that made Grace Jacoby's heart sing—they often went riding in the park after school and then went off to Suggie's. When they returned to their separate apartments, they smelled bitter and aromatic, of horse and pepperoni.

Imelda did not live in, but a room in the nether part of the Jacobys' apartment was hers, in which she sometimes entertained her brother, who drank quantities of tomato juice. His name was Francisco and he was an ensign in the Colombian navy, but on the side he smuggled a little cocaine into the United States in gift bags of coffee beans. It was quite a lucrative sideline and he had set Imelda up in an apartment in Washington Heights, wither she retired after a day with the Jacobys. In the apartment lived Francisco, when he was on shore leave, Imelda, and her fiancé, Freddy Bonafia, who played the tenor saxophone in Graucho Pacheco's Latin Band.

It was at a concert in the Bronx Music Palace that Jane Cather-

ine and Tito saw Imelda in her street clothes. She was almost un-
recognizable. At the Jacobys she wore a black uniform and black
sneakers, and stuck her hair into a bright-green snood. Her skin
was the color of cork, and she had beige eyes. There was quite a
lot of gold in her smile. At the Bronx Music Palace she wore a
dress of electric blue with matching shoes. She was very thin, but
her dress was cut so close to the bone that it was difficult to imagine how she managed to walk. Her hair, out of its snood, was arranged in a series of curls decorated with blue velvet bows. When
she saw Tito and Jane Catherine, she gave them a bright but
vague smile. On one side of her sat Francisco; on the other was
Wilda Bonafia, Freddy's sister, wearing what looked like a series
of silver hair nets.

The music began, and Tito knocked Jane Catherine in the ribs,
and Jane Catherine knocked him back—a sign that they liked
what they heard. Several overexcited members of the audience
shouted in Spanish that to Tito sounded like highly inflected running water.

The Bronx Music Palace was immense, cavernous, and moist.
Even a standing-room-only crowd seemed minuscule and lost in
its depths, but the acoustics were perfect. Jane Catherine and Tito
held hands. Jane Catherine was musically emotional and Graucho
Pacheco's band was so good that she found herself in tears. He
was only the first act, and by the time Jocko Sanagustino came
on, she was practically beside herself.

Tito was a genius, not that he cared much. At
his school he had a large desk, rather like that of a nineteenth-
century merchant, on which he kept a conch shell, a potted plant,
and a small cactus. He spent a good deal of time staring at these
objects, or gazing out the window.

"I have to let my brain cool off," he explained, having discovered that two hours of work on his part was worth ten on anybody
else's.

Jane Catherine's high level-brain worked at a steadier, less
manic pace, but she too needed frequent rest and rehabilitation.

She kept a transistor radio plug in her ear, and turned on some music between calculus problems. On a dare, without much effort, she had memorized the first book of *Paradise Lost,* and had constructed a DNA molecule out of shirt cardboard.

Under the well-known guise of studying together, Jane Catherine and Tito rubbed each other's backs behind closed doors and listened to the music they loved the best. Tito was teaching Jane Catherine Spanish.

"What are they singing about?" she asked.

"It's about a coffee pot," said Tito. "It's the South American mentality. They sing about beaches and bars of soap."

In the kitchen, meanwhile, Imelda basted the chicken. Then she read, and holding the book, her face took on the seriousness of a Chinese scholar. She sat straight in her chair, her neck stiff. Her eyes were steely and intense in back of wire frame glasses that made all her features seem immobile with effort. She was reading a novel of horror, featuring a monster called El Gordo.

Jane Catherine's closest friend was Leah Morrisy, and their loving admiration had been originally based on self-assumed uniqueness. They were stylistically different, but the intensity of their styles was similarly motivated. Basically, they thought their personalities were works of art, and they were not far wrong.

Leah's true love was Mick Skipworth, a blond, slightly wall-eyed National Science Foundation winner: he had mutated fruit flies. Her family lived in a townhouse, on the third floor of which she had a room cluttered with her secret possessions: a cheap nightie with a plunging décolletage, from a mail-order house in Hollywood; a leather jacket, stolen by Mick from his older brother; a set of spangled pasties; some hot, illiterate love letters, and an old briefcase filled with sultry, sulky photographs of herself, taken by Mick and several previous loves.

Leah was tiny, skinny, and her eyes were so brown they appeared to have no pupils, giving her the smoldering look of a burning tire. She was shaped on the lines of a vase and she was heavily addicted to Coca-Cola. For her birthday, Mick gave her a case of it, and it was gone within five days. Her hair was dramatically shaggy and waiflike.

Her mother said of her with a sigh: "I'm afraid to let her out on the street. She walks from her pelvic bones. My heart fails when she leaves for school, even in that uniform."

                Some afternoons, Leah and Jane Catherine walked through Central Park, wearing ritual clothing. Jane Catherine wore the hacking jacket that had been her mother's twenty years ago, loafers with tassels, and bright-green socks. The belt that held up her jeans was a present from Tito. Leah wore an old shocking pink windbreaker that had never been washed—she had bought it second-hand for half a dollar and taken it to her heart. She wore black velvet trousers, a pair of minuscule ballet slippers, and a fifty-dollar shirt.

"I'd like to turn Mick into an ice cream soda," she said. "He has the most beautiful mouth I've ever seen. His brother is a moron and his parents are awful. He calls them the gargoyles. His mother cries all the time. He comes in, and she cries. He goes out, and she cries. He goes to play soccer and she's in tears and when he won that science thing, she almost fell apart." Leah yawned. "She hates me. She thinks I'm cheap. She told Micky. She said: That little bit dresses like a tiny French tart."

"Nobody's mother talks that way," said Jane Catherine.

"I made it up," Leah said. "But that's what she would say if she had a mind. They're all so brainless over there. Micky says he feels like a changeling. His sister Florence has begun to call herself Flopsy. It's depressing."

"Tito's parents are invisible," said Jane Catherine. "Or else we're invisible to them."

"That's because you dress nice," said Leah, pulling her cerise jacket around her. "Someday Tito and Mick will be memory."

"I only think of that when I want to make myself cry."

"Well, I think about it all the time and it makes me seasick. We'll all go off to college and be memories. We'll say: remember

Tito? Remember Micky? God only knows what will become of us."

"What will, do you think?" Jane Catherine said.

"I think no one will know what to do with us. We have too many tastes for our age, but it'll get worse. People will call us strange—it'll be our prefix. People will take you out to nice civilized parties and you'll come home and put the old record player on. People will say I'm cheap, or some variation of that. I'm a prisoner of my sultriness. I'll wear these kind of clothes, and so will you and only very odd, intense men will find us at all interesting."

They walked past the boulders and toward the fountain where they saw Imelda holding the arm of an unnaturally tall, skinny man wearing green lizard cowboy boots and a ten-gallon hat. Next to him, Imelda was a peg. She had on a bright-pink dress that was as small as a scarf. She looked like a little flag that fluttered off his belt. When she saw Jane Catherine she smiled her unnerving, gold smile.

Jane Catherine was abashed. She was frightened of Imelda, who made her feel profoundly awkward. She did not approve of having servants and did not know how to deal with them. The Jacobys, who instilled in their children the belief that servants are human beings, did what all parents do: they treated their servants like human beings who are deaf, or blind, or suffering from some other lowering infirmity. The recently deceased old Suzie they had treated like a kindly grandmother from another planet, whose customs were not their customs—with the courtesy they would have doled out to a dignitary from an underdeveloped country.

But Imelda was named for a song on the Zaida label, sung by Los Graduados. It was a song Jane Catherine and Tito danced to for hours in the privacy of Jane Catherine's room. Had it not been for Imelda, this pleasure would have been unknown to them. Besides, Imelda was the genuine product, and Jane Catherine felt embarrassed about her record collection, her Spanish comic books, as if her love were simply poaching; that no matter how sincere her rapture at the Bronx Music Palace, she was slightly fraudulent.

Jane Catherine approached Imelda shyly, and asked her in self-conscious Spanish how she did. Leah stood beside her, slouching on the famous pelvic bones. Imelda held on to her young man, who Jane Catherine knew was Freddy Bonafia.

"You have an espanish boyfreng," Imelda said, and then was silent. Since no one could find anything to say, they indulged in a spate of handshaking all around. Imelda had on a small diamond ring. She smiled at Freddy and they walked away.

Leah and Jane Catherine walked to the lake and watched the boats.

"Sometimes I can't talk to anyone," Jane Catherine said. There were tears in her eyes.

"Don't get overwrought."

"She had a ring on. She's probably getting married. She'll quit and I never even spoke to her."

"What did you want her to tell you?"

"I didn't want her to tell me anything," said Jane Catherine. "I just wanted to talk to her. Tito and I used to see her at the Music Palace and it always made me feel terrible and out of place."

"Democracy is hard on everyone," Leah said. "Remember Niles? I can't even remember his last name. He was from the Roberts-Arco driving school. He was my driving teacher but he wanted to be a cop. We used to go up to Van Cortlandt Park and kiss. When I got my license, that was that. But he called to find out if I passed my driving test."

"It's just that the world seems to be divided between Imelda and those rotten Bieberman twins," said Jane Catherine, "and I'm on the wrong side."

"You're not on any side. You're a mutant, and so am I," Leah said.

"Tito is a free-lance," said Jane Catherine. "For a genius, he's sort of a blockhead. He doesn't have any sentimental memory. When I think that a day is over and will never repeat, I get all ropy inside, but Tito thinks that life is a string that pulls you along."

They pulled their jackets tighter.

"Who knows," said Leah. "It probably is."

      Imelda's token room at the Jacobys' was as bare as a bone, but her room in Washington Heights was another matter altogether. An enormous poster of Graucho and the band covered one wall. Over the bed hung a stuffed alligator, an enormous one. Affixed to its snout was a pair of sunglasses. Freddy's numerous cowboy boots decorated the floor, singly and in pairs. They had three-inch heels, which brought his height up to six six. He was thin as a ruler and his trousers would have all been too short for him had not Imelda made him ornamental cuffs out of multicolored velvet. She and Freddy were fond of multicolored velvet. The bedspread was made of it, and one wall was covered with it.

Together they had grandiose, technicolor dreams of domestic architecture: of a house built on stilts with a gabled roof made of bottles; of a coffee table made of a kettle drum; of a floor that was real grass. They wanted two babies called Flute and Cymba. They wanted a sequoia tree to bisect their living room. They were happy and visual. Two days after Imelda told Mrs. Jacoby in incomprehensible English that she was quitting, she and Freddy were married and pictures of their wedding appeared in the papers.

Jane Catherine kept the clippings. She sent Imelda a bottle of champagne and the Jacobys sent an ornate silver candy dish, of the kind sent to distant cousins.

Jane Catherine walked unhappily around Imelda's old pantry room. There was nothing in it but the furniture and some dust. She sat in the armchair and contemplated her future: in the summer, she and Leah were going to take a course at the Université de Grenoble given for high school students, and they had fought hard for the privilege.

"How can I let her go?" Mrs. Morrisy had agonized to her husband. "Alvin, how can I let her loose among the French? Oh,

God, these kids. Why can't they just go to tennis camp, like everyone else?"

Mrs. Jacoby sighed as Jane Catherine procured six pairs of bluejeans for the event, and encrusted the cuffs of three of them with ten rows of solid buttons. Leah bought a pair of orange ballet slippers to wear on the boat across. Micky was going to Woods Hole to wash bottles for a marine biologist and Tito was going to his father's horse farm in Argentina. Jane Catherine felt her lightness collapse. She thought of what she would pack to keep her happy in France: the belt Tito had given her, one of his socks, a little blue plush vampire bat. She knew that she was storing up memories the way the rich collect paintings. She knew that making memories was the same as making history. But it didn't matter: she was crying anyway. Some day, she knew, this room, this time, Tito and Imelda, herself as she was now, would all be memory and it filled her with pain and tenderness. When she finished crying, she called Leah, who had been crying too. They met in the park and walked slowly downtown, to shop for what Leah called "trash items."

"It's cosmic," said Leah. "But it's also because we're precocious."

"Pretty soon we won't even be that," said Jane Catherine. "Pretty soon you and I will be talking about how dear and touching we were then, which is now, only later. It's very dislocating to think about."

They sighed the light, profound sighs of adolescence and locked arms, since they were still young enough to do so. They walked without speaking, feeling very sage. Their steps were careful and precise, and as they walked toward the street and into the crowd, they knew that they were only two little girls, strolling past a line of trees.

 children, dogs, and
desperate men

At an engagement party for her cousin Tom and Katie Rosenstatt, the art historian's daughter, Elizabeth Bayard met a man called Richard Mignon. At the time of her introduction, she was sitting on the sofa with one of the innumerable Rosenstatt nephews asleep by her side, and Tom's spaniel asleep on her feet.

"Are you always barricaded by small fry?" said Richard Mignon, looking down at her. "I'm the well-known drunken cartographer. You're Tom's cousin and you write about music."

"I've never met a cartographer before," said Elizabeth. "Not even a sober one."

"The drunken ones are better. We're a very small, exclusive circle. We also do wine tasting. Care for a snort?"

She held her glass out, and he filled it up. At first glance, he looked like a boy who has seen catastrophe, but on second look, he was a slightly wrecked, boyish man on the fringes of middle age. His eyes were blue and as wide as plates and his hair was thick, curly, and graying. He had taken off his jacket and his shirttail hung out. When the nephew had been taken off by his mother for a formal nap, Richard sat down, squashing Elizabeth into a corner.

"Do you think there's a causal connection between wine consumption and cartography?" she said.

"Oh, absolutely," said Richard Mignon. "My maps are all guesswork. Ancient cities, lost cities, places they only have accounts of. It takes me out of the real world. I can't be expected to cope."

"You might use the subway guide as inspirational reading."

"I've considered it, believe me," he said. "But as far as wine goes, these art historians always have the best, so I like to soak it up while I can."

"Situational gluttony," said Elizabeth.

"How well you understand these things," Richard Mignon said.

Tom Bayard was crazy about his cousin and he followed her the way you listen to a symphony with the score on your lap. To him she was serious, level-headed, and smart, but Elizabeth, who was recovering from an unhappy love affair, saw herself as shaken and out of place. She did not fall in love often, and when she did, she depended on what Tom called "refined instinct." Since she knew she was generally good-natured and cheerful, she was a little surprised at how long it was taking for her heart to mend, but her instinct had played her false, and that gave her cause for serious and painful thought. The less complicated side of her nature was clear to children, who adored her, and animals, who generally took bread at her hand.

At the end of the evening, she and Richard Mignon shared a taxi downtown. He had consumed about two bottles of wine and behaved with the sloppy, affectionate dignity of a large dog, and held her hand as if it were an eggshell. She expected he would keep the cab, but instead he paid the driver and walked her to her door.

"If I don't get some coffee, I'm going to fall down the stairs," he said, looking rattled and sad. "I know it's terribly late."

He inspected her books while she made the coffee, and told her she was a beacon of kindness. He balanced the cup on his knees until the coffee was cold, and then drank it in two gulps.

"Are we fated to meet only at engagement parties, or could we have dinner together?" he said.

"No."

"No what? No dinner, or not only at parties?"

"No dinner."

"Is there something about me you find apelike and disgusting?"

"You're married," said Elizabeth.

"Bless my soul," said Richard Mignon. "You don't often hear that in this day and age. Well, you're a very sweet girl to have put up with me, drunken as I am." He gave her a courtly kiss in the vicinity of her forehead, put on his coat, and walked unsteadily down the stairs.

Two days later she received an elaborate note, in italic hand, apologizing for alcoholic behavior and inviting her to a publication party at the Renaissance Club for a book called *The Structure of Renaissance Florence*. He had done the maps. The postscript said: "Please, please be there."

Elizabeth put her feet up on her desk and studied the note. It was written on thick, cream-colored paper. She showed it to Tom.

"What am I supposed to make of this?" she said.

"He thinks you're an attractive, intelligent girl and he wants you to come to his party."

"But if I go, Tom, he'll think I'm flirting with him."

"It's not against the law to flirt," Tom said.

"It's pretty high on my list of sins," said Elizabeth. "What's the story on him?"

"Katie says he's married to a harpsichordist and they have six daughters or five sons. A lot of kids. He's known for his bumptious charm."

"But if I go to this party, it'll look as if I want him to come around."

"Elizabeth, you have more scruples than the Book of Common Prayer. He's a nice fellow. You obviously find him interesting enough to think about. This doesn't put you on the line. Why don't you just go?"

"I don't like slight connections," said Elizabeth. "These things don't speak well of me. Look at George."

George was George Garzanti. He was a physicist, and the year before, he and Elizabeth had fallen in love at explosive first sight. They had met at a Christmas party and had been almost inseparable for about six months. There was no way, it seemed, in which they did not fit. Her best articles had been written at his kitchen table. They sat side by side, knees touching, in the library, looking up from their books to smile rhapsodically. George thought it was miraculous that they had met at all. These months filled Elizabeth with a joy intense enough to cause suspicion: nothing that luminous and sharp could last. George was recently divorced. He was moody and frenetic. Elizabeth waited for their situation to calm down, for some comfortable normalcy in which they could both relax, but George lived at a skittish and eruptive pace. He invented crises. He drove himself. Even his moments of concentrated tenderness were unnerving, followed as they were by panic and frenzy. It was hit and run.

Finally, there was a showdown. Love was getting in the way of work, George said, and since she didn't want obligation to fill the slot of affection, she let herself into his apartment one afternoon, collected her books, and left on his desk the books and clothing he had left at her apartment. Then she hung her set of keys on a hook by the door, and left, locking herself out.

She assumed that it was over, but George, who could not find a way of incorporating her into his life, was not about to let her go. He wrote and phoned, but he had no emotional vocabulary to explain his feelings with, and finally she asked him not to call.

The night before the publication party, the telephone rang and it was George. He said he had had a terrible dream about her, and wanted to know if she was all right. It knocked her backward to hear from him. She told him again not to call, and then cried herself to sleep.

The Renaissance Club was a series of formal rooms in a mansion off Madison Avenue. People moved from room to room, leaving their drinks on Florentine tables. A flat band of smoke extended above their heads. Elizabeth lounged against the wall, waiting for Richard Mignon, or anyone else she knew. The wall opposite her was mirrored and when she looked across, she saw herself in a silk dress, her ashy hair brushed to a shine, grinning. Then she spotted him. He was surrounded, and the strain of politesse looked as if it was strangling him. He was holding a glass of wine, standing sideways, restless, anxious to get over to her, gesturing.

Finally he was free, and dragged two chairs next to the window. "Are you very bored?" he said.

"No. I always like looking around," said Elizabeth.

"A lot of old stiffs here," he said.

"If you don't see all that many stiffs, it's kind of a thrill."

"You're making fun of me," he said. "Why am I the target of everyone's mirth?"

"It's probably because your socks don't match," said Elizabeth. He looked at his feet. One sock was green and the other gray. "I feel as if I'd been here for several months. I don't have to stay. Let's have a quick dinner."

He did most of the talking over the meal, and Elizabeth surveyed him. His charm was obviously the result of considerable cultivation, but it worked. Besides, there was something about him that was as innocent as a kitten, and he seemed to be perennially baffled. After dinner they found themselves cramped into another taxi.

"This guy is trying to kill us," he said, grabbing her shoulder, as the cab hurtled down the West Side highway.

Once in her apartment, they were as tentative as adolescents. In a crowd, he was civilization itself, but faced alone with a girl he was abashed, and it was contagious. They drank wine standing up in front of her fireplace, and they talked about the Renaissance Club. It was not what Elizabeth wanted to hear: she wanted to know about his home life, and what lead him to be standing in her apartment, and why his wife hadn't come to his publication party, but he kept such a tight rein on his conversation that any personal interjection would have been inappropriate, almost rude. When he finished his wine, he wound his muffler around his neck. It was midnight. She wondered if he were going to kiss her, and if so, how he would go about it.

Like a boy at the end of a prom, he kissed her at the door, holding her by the elbows. It was a light, shy, boyish kiss.

Then he looked at her intently. "Say something," he said.

"This is meant to be a sin," she said.

"Kissing?"

"Kissing a married man."

He gave her a puzzled, dismissing look and then held her so close she felt that she was being impaled by the buttons on his Chesterfield. Then he gently pushed her away. She opened the door.

"If there were another boring party to invite you to, I would, but there isn't. I hope I'll see you anyway," he said, and left.

Sometimes Elizabeth thought she would never get over George Garzanti, that he would stay with her like a splinter, sleeping under the skin. She wanted a life that was clear and straightforward, that made sense. George was like a tornado, or a random act of God.

That night, she thought of Richard Mignon. It was a balm of sorts to have a man pay court to her, but was she to Richard Mignon what George had been to her, urging on something she had no intention of fulfilling?

They met again, at a large, formal dinner party. The Rosenstatts were there, and Tom and Katie. Richard Mignon introduced her to his wife, Violet, whose dry hand she shook. It was a large enough party to get lost in: there were a series of tables and she was separated from him by the length of the room. After dinner, she sat with Tom, and Justin Rosenstatt, Katie's cousin. Richard Mignon stopped her at the door as she was leaving.

"Are you going, so soon?" he said.

"I've got work to do," she said.

"We must see each other again," he said.

She left in a kind of despair. George Garzanti occurred to her, sitting at his kitchen table, barefoot. Thinking about the intimacy they had constructed gave her a sense of loss as dizzying and palpable as an earthquake.

Outside, she breathed the icy air and realized that, for all her high-mindedness, she was curious to see how far Richard Mignon would go, how much effort he would make on her behalf. She knew exactly what her limit was, and, probably, what she and Richard Mignon needed was an emotional clinch, something to wrap some withered or disappointed affections around. They would cling to each other some night, worked up to a misguided longing, and turn it down in the name of honor and good sense.

Saturday afternoon, Tom and Katie appeared, bringing Becky, the spaniel, who was snappish from being in the park. Her paws were covered with shredded leaves. They dragged three armchairs in front of the fire and had coffee. Becky paced and snarled, and finally jumped into Elizabeth's lap, where she slept for the rest of the afternoon, leaving Elizabeth covered with dog hairs. Tom said:

"You seem to have captured Mignon's heart."

"I haven't captured anything."

"He's always talking to you," said Katie.

"Is it noticeable?" Elizabeth said.

"It isn't noticeable to the general public," said Tom. "But I'm for it, since this is the first time I've seen you in really good spirits since George."

They leashed Becky and walked into the hall. "Because you are in fabulous spirits," Tom said. "You really are."

Elizabeth trusted Tom. She was mindful of her mental states, but she knew she was broadcasting something she was not aware of. She stood in front of the mirror trying to see how her fabulous spirits were manifesting themselves. The face in the mirror was grinning faintly.

On Sunday afternoon, Richard Mignon called her. "I'm right near you," he said. "Can I stop by, if you're not busy?"

"I'm not busy," Elizabeth said. Outside it was bleak and foggy. From her window, the trees looked wet and gray, and the air was as thick as woodsmoke. She sat in front of the fire, toasting her feet.

The clothes he wore to visit were the clothes he always wore: elegant, but askew. He maintained a form of battered dandyism. He hung up his coat and sat down. She poured him a glass of sherry. The level of awkwardness in the room was dense. She threw another log on the fire and they embarked upon a scattered, unfocused conversation. When it was scarcely bearable, she went into the kitchen to make herself a cup of tea, and when she came back he was asleep. He had simply turned his head toward the crook of the chair and gone to sleep as easily as a child. He looked boyish and effortless. He was not being sociable, charming, or socially competent, but only asleep.

It was a comfort to have him there. It had begun to sleet. Ice sprinkled against the windows. It was calm and enclosed, the sort of day she loved.

"I've never been calm before," said George Garzanti, long ago. "Only with you. You are the most level person I have ever met." The thought of it was like a stitch in her side.

Richard Mignon woke himself up by shrugging his shoulders. Before he could collect himself, he smiled. Then he was horrified.

"Please don't be apologetic," Elizabeth said. "Everyone falls asleep in that chair when there's a fire."

He looked at his watch and scowled. "God, I'm boring. I come to visit you and I fall asleep. Now I've got to go."

They stood up at the same time, and he took her hands. He looked tired and mournful. "Do I get to kiss you at the door?" he asked.

"Yes you get to kiss me at the door."

"We're very sociable, aren't we?"

He kissed her on the forehead, and went down the stairs.

That night she went to Tom's to fix his typewriter. She had small hands, mechanical ability, and an interest in machines. Two of the keys were stuck and she fixed them with a tweezer.

On the way home, she stopped at an all-night grocery store to buy some milk. The aisles were filled with children. A little boy wearing yellow mittens and a snow suit was wandering among the shelves of biscuits.

"Hey," he said to Elizabeth.

"Hey what?"

"Could you reach me those animal crackers?" They were on the top shelf.

"I like the tigers," said the little boy when she put the package in his hands. "This is a bear. In the winter they go into their house and they don't come out till it gets to be springtime." She was kneeling beside him, and they were head to head, examining the box. His mother, a blonde in a seal coat, appeared at the end of the aisle.

"Come on, Giles. I've been looking for you." She looked at Elizabeth as if confronting a known kidnapper. "Your brothers are waiting. Now put those cookies back."

"I can't reach, Mommy."

"Giles, darling, you musn't go about picking up people. Now say goodbye to the lady who was nice to you." She pulled him by the mitten.

"Bye bye. Thank you," he said.

Elizabeth paid for the milk, and realized, after discarding several possibilities, that the woman was Violet Mignon.

Richard Mignon rang her doorbell the following Wednesday. It was snowing and he was wearing a ten-gallon hat.

"I never drop by," he said. "But then, I never expected to find you home. I was right around the corner. I actually don't like it when people ring my doorbell."

"Are you going to make a speech or come in?"

It was late, and she was tired. The article she had been working on was going badly and lay abandoned on her desk.

"What can I give you?" she said.

"I wish I knew."

In the apartment across the hall, someone was playing the recorder. It was like the hum of a machine, thin, reedy, and monotonous. He untied the ribbon holding back her hair and watched it spill to her shoulders, turning her toward the light as if she were part of a still life he was arranging.

"I don't know what I want," he said. His hands were on her shoulders.

"You better cut it out," Elizabeth said. "I have the weakest flesh in town."

"I don't know what that means," he said, looking steadily at her.

"It means I'm very vulnerable, and this is unsuitable."

"You let me in," he said.

She looked back into his intelligent, catlike face.

"I'm very polite," she said. "I try to keep my life in order, I like to know that what I do makes sense. I don't understand what sense this makes."

He stood as formally as a young Prussian soldier about to present her with a bouquet, but his face was relaxed, lazy, and grinning. Quietly he stroked her bright hair.

"Are you dismissing me?" he said.

"In a way."

"Does that mean if I call you you won't speak to me?"

"No."

"Then I'll phone you up," he said.

Katie's cousin Justin taught history at Columbia. He was in his middle thirties and had been divorced. His wife had left him with a kitchen full of French cooking ware, whose existence he justified by going once a week to a cooking school run by a German lady poet who had been at Cordon Bleu. Every few months he gave a small dinner party to announce one of his culinary triumphs, and he liked to mix his friends. At the last of these, Elizabeth had sat next to a Southern lawyer who wrote tone poems. His name was Terry Parmett, and over the pears he had said: "Do you have a lovah?" And when she asked him why he wanted to know, he said: "If you don't, it seems to me a real waste of lovely flesh."

The next time she went to one of Justin's dinners, Terry Parmett was there.

"Katie and Tom were supposed to come, but they had to go to New Haven," Justin said, "so it's just us."

"You git better looking every time I see you," said Terry. He had a snub nose, eyes full of manic inertia, and glasses that seemed either too big or too small for him.

"You've only seen me once," Elizabeth said.

He drank a good deal of Bourbon before dinner, and a lot of wine during it. After dinner, Justin, who was compulsively neat, took the dishes to the kitchen. Elizabeth heard the sound of running water. Terry Parmett slumped toward her, looking as if he would melt onto the table.

"I'd give an awful lot to know you," he said.

"I'll give you my social security number."

"You know what I mean. I find you quite delectable, but I think that if I called you up, you'd mock me. But I could get quite het up over you."

"That's very flattering."

"I'd give a lot," he said. "You have no idea how fine I think you are. I'm quite degenerate, you know."

Elizabeth said, "I'm sorry to hear it."

"What I mean is, what would you say if I offered you money. For your favors." It was so outrageous she laughed.

"How much?" she said.

"Ten thousand dollars," he said. "That would be about my limit, but I'm extremely wealthy, as Justin will tell you."

"That's quite a come-on."

He took out his checkbook and put it on the table. "I keep a running balance," he said coldly. "It's all there. I give you the check, you call the bank."

"Enough," said Elizabeth.

"I'm quite serious," Terry Parmett said.

As they were leaving, Elizabeth took Justin aside. "Your pal Terry is a maniac. Can I trust him to get me a taxi?"

"He's drunk," said Justin. "Wild but harmless. He'll get you a taxi. Southerners are always polite."

The night was full of cold, gray fog. The traffic lights blinked woozy red and green. The cars, as they passed, lit up a snow flurry. As they turned the corner, Terry said:

"We're being followed."

"You're being silly."

"We *are* being followed," Terry said. "Turn around."

Out of the corner of her eye, Elizabeth saw a man stalking close to a building. Then he raced across the sidewalk, and crouched by a parked car. He crept into the street, flattened himself against a truck, and darted over to a mailbox. Elizabeth squinted through the fog. It was George Garzanti, wearing his old leather jacket. They were three blocks from his apartment. His eyes met hers and glared like a cat's, caught by a torch. He moved under a streetlight and stood illuminated, snow falling on his shoulders. He looked pained, and crazy.

"Get me a cab," Elizabeth said to Terry and as they walked to the corner, she saw George watch, move forward, and then turn and walk the other way.

"Are you going to let me come home with you?" Terry asked.

"Does that mean can you see me home?"

"No. It means can I stay with you."

"No."

"Then I'm not interested. Here's your cab."

When she got home, there was a note on her mailbox that said:

I came by to see you, but obviously you were out. Call me at Ox 3-5727 between nine and twelve and tell me when I can see you.

Richard Mignon

She walked up the stairs, tearing the note into tiny pieces that fluttered behind her like confetti.

 wet

LUCY WAS A BORN SWIMMER: she had been in the water as an infant and swam without water wings by the time she was three. At five, she was swimming underwater with ease and began to practice diving when she was six.

Her family lived in St. Paul and spent the summers in a cedar-shingled house at Stone Boy Lake. A set of steps led from the house to the dock. The lake was a mile long, ringed by dense, moss-sided firs and overshadowed by hills of timber. It was almost gothically dark, except at high noon when the sun cut straight down onto the water like the beam of a klieg light. It was so quiet that if you swam early in the morning all you would hear was the sound of your own splashing. At Stone Boy Lake, you swam to your friends, and it was not uncommon for Lucy to swim several miles a day. The summer people kept towels waiting on their docks.

In the winter, Lucy swam in the pool of Mallard Academy in St. Paul. In the East, at college, she swam through the seasons, through exams, through love affairs. She was in the water the morning of her marriage to Carl Wilmott, keeping her scarfed head up so as not to ruin her wedding hairdo.

Carl and Lucy had met in Boston, and were married three years later in the summer house on Stone Boy Lake. They lived in a light, sparse apartment in Cambridge. The wooden floors were highly polished and the furniture was so trim and modern that it looked as if it would skim across the room if pushed. Lucy worked for the law review, and Carl had an assistantship in the history department, but when he was offered a position in Chicago, they decided to take it, packed, and were ready to move within a week. Neither went in much for heavy baggage or personal artifacts. They liked what could be easily carried. Their only decorations were a Peruvian wall rug, two Appalachian quilts, a watercolor of Boston Common in the 1880's, and a soapstone seal, carved by Eskimos. Three days after New Year's, they flew to Chicago and were settled the next day.

Lucy was middle-sized and lean. Her features were small, but craggy, as if they had been reduced to human scale from some large, rough-hewn monument. When she smiled, her eyes almost disappeared behind her cheekbones and her skin was so translucently white you could see the veins beneath it.

Carl, who was ruddy and large, was often stricken at the thought of her fragility, and he was constantly amazed by her ruggedness. His sports were handball and squash—he liked to sweat and strain—and he watched with wonder as his delicate wife dove from boulders into mountain pools so cold they shocked his entire body if he put so much as a foot in. She raced into the ocean at Maine in October while he sat shivering on the beach wearing double sweaters. He watched her slide down waterfalls in Vermont, her hair tangled by white water.

The first day in Chicago, Carl went to a faculty meeting, while Lucy unpacked the last two cartons and then called University Information to find out where she could swim. There was a pool, she was told, at McWerter Hall, nine blocks away.

It was below freezing. She could feel the cold through her boots. It had been ten years since she had lived in this kind of weather, and her body had forgotten. The inside of her nose was stiff. By the time she reached McWerter Hall her feet felt like stones.

The guard pointed the way to the ladies' locker room, where she filled out forms for an official pass and was given a temporary card stamped "new faculty." The pool was empty except for two girls who sat on the side in dry bathing suits, dangling their feet in the water. Their voices murmured and echoed. When they laughed, it sounded like distant gun shot.

Lucy dove off the high board and swam a lap under water. When she surfaced, she was alone, and she swam by herself for two hours. In the locker room, she combed her lank hair in front of the foggy mirror, and by the time she got home, even with a hat and scarf, the front of her hair was frozen.

In February, it snowed, and then got colder. Coal trucks unloaded in the streets, turning the ice black, and children coming home from school skated on jet-colored humps that formed in the middle of the streets. They played with their heads down and walked backward against the wind. People passed each other with their eyes streaming. When the wind let up, they brushed the tears off with their gloves, as if suffering from secret heartbreak.

Carl hated the cold, but he and Lucy liked Chicago. Their new apartment was very much like the one they had had in Cambridge —light and sparse. A small set of people they had known at college formed the beginning of their social life. Carl was making friends in the department, and Lucy, who was job hunting, explored the neighborhood.

After his two o'clock class, Carl usually had coffee with Johnny Esterhazy, who had gone to high school and college with him. They were both New Yorkers and the cold exhausted them.

"I saw Lucy on the street yesterday," Johnny said. "I thought I was coming down with terminal frostbite, but she looked like the breath of spring."

"She's the old original polar bear," said Carl. "She grew up in St. Paul, which is the arctic circle, as far as I'm concerned."

"Well, I admire her," said Johnny. "Her bangs were frozen."

"You admire her because her bangs were frozen?"

"What I mean is, it takes real fortitude to swim in this kind of weather. It takes courage to even *walk* in this kind of weather. I told her I thought she was crazy, but she said she'd been in the pool almost every day since you came here."

Carl drank his coffee in silence and watched a group of girls go by, so swaddled in their layers of clothing they could hardly walk. He knew Lucy loved to swim: she swam all summer, but it surprised him to know she swam in the winter, too. The fact that she had gone swimming every day since they had come to Chicago and had never said a word about it left him speechless. He had no idea where the university pool was, and thought of asking Johnny, but it seemed to him that asking was an admission of some terrible ignorance. How could he not know such an elementary fact about his own wife?

Walking home, he decided to confront her, but he could not arrange a question that was neither accusatory nor whimpering, and he could not articulate the source of his pain. Was it that she swam, or that she didn't tell him? Lucy had been swimming all her life: it was a perfectly natural thing for her to do, but he was suffering nonetheless.

She was in the kitchen when he came in. Her hair wasn't wet. It didn't smell of chlorine. Her face was cool when she kissed him, as it always was. They sat down to a large, cheering dinner, after which they stretched out on the sofa and read. It was normal life. At midnight, they yawned, and with their arms around each other, went to bed.

In March, the cold began to crack and the black ice softened, forming deep, muddy puddles. When it snowed, the snow was light and fine. Then it sleeted, and by April it only rained. Tiny green swells began to appear on the stunted hedges.

Finally, it was clear, cold prairie spring. Lucy walked toward Lake Michigan. The grass in the park was brown and scorched, and the bridle path was as wet as a creek. Clouds of mist embraced the Museum of Science and Industry. She walked across the bridge above the Outer Drive and onto the rocks by the lake.

Under her bluejeans, sweater, and coat she was wearing a bathing suit, and in her book bag was a beach towel. Johnny Esterhazy had told her that Lake Michigan was polluted, but it was clear enough so that she could see the rocks beneath the water and the swaying beards of algae on their sides. Whatever it had in it, it did not have chlorine. She stripped to her bathing suit and the wind smacked her like a fist.

There was not a soul around. She climbed from rock to rock until she was standing in water up to her knees, and then she jumped.

Over dinner, Lucy and Carl talked about the casual, easy shape their life was taking. Johnny Esterhazy and his fiancée were coming to dinner on Friday. The head of the history department had invited them to a cocktail party. Lucy had an interview at the law library. Ted and Ellie Lifter, a pair of sociologists who lived downstairs, had asked them for coffee and dessert.

They reviewed the events of their day, and wondered whether to get orchestra or box seats for the Chicago symphony. But Lucy never said anything about swimming, and Carl knew that in some way he had overreacted. Swimming to Lucy was like breathing, and did she report to him that she had breathed all day?

When he looked at her across the dinner table, her pale, fair hair and skin, her pale eyes, and the vein that divided her forehead, he looked for any sign of deception, but there was nothing but openness and affection. He looked into her steady, unblinking eyes and tried to see if she was capable of duplicity, but every feature in her face was loving, straightforward, and direct.

At night, her long thighs were cool and the insides of her arms were cold. As she slept, Carl thought how fragile she appeared, and how tough she actually was. It occurred to his sleepy mind that this was a deception in itself. At times, he was overwhelmed that she was purposely shutting him out of a part of her life, and then, suddenly, it all seemed normal to him. If he asked her, she would smile her eye-diminishing smile and tell him of course she swam every day. But he did not ask, and could not. He could not bear to admit that what was second nature to her had been news to him. He fluctuated between panic and calm. If she was swimming every day in Chicago, it meant that she had done the same in Cambridge—all that time and she had never said a word, but had simply arranged a part of her life away from him and gone swimming in it.

In the summers they went to his parents in Maine, or to hers on Stone Boy Lake, and swam together. But usually they were apart for most of the day, and she spent several hours of it in secret. It seemed so deliberate, so concealed and contrived—it broke his heart to think about it. But then perhaps his vision was distorted. They had been together for five years and he knew her swimming was something she probably assumed he took for granted, but at night it looked like sabotage.

On the day of a heavy rainstorm, he saw her from the window of his office, walking under a golf umbrella toward McWerter Hall, and he followed her. He climbed the stairs to the bleachers and waited until she came through a door and walked to the edge of the pool. His jacket was glazed with mist and he was sweating under his collar. The roots of his hair were damp. Through the steam and haze, he saw his wife on the low board. She dove into the water like a bird and he could see the white streak of her gliding to the shallow end. He wanted to call out, but held himself back, and since she didn't look up, she never saw him. She tossed her hair out of her eyes and he could see that they were slightly unfocused by chlorine.

There was a catch in his throat as he watched her walk the perimeter of the pool, leaving delicate footprints on the tiles. She stood on the tip of the high board, and when she connected with the water it seemed to slice his heart.

She did a swan dive, then a jackknife. Stifling in his tweed, he watched ten laps of her sleek, racing crawl. Then she climbed back on the high board, framed by a window the width of the room. The sky was the color of faded ink. His clothes itched and he longed to throw them off and dive in with her. But it would have been betrayal. Instead, he watched her do a half-gainer and when she was underwater, he left by the side door.

After dinner, he said abruptly: "I want to go swimming with you tomorrow." He was that desperate.

Lucy smiled and her cheekbones hid her eyes. It was a truly open smile.

"Sure," she said. "That would be nice. I'm going around three thirty. Is that O.K. for you?"

"It's fine."

That was the end of the conversation: the spell was broken. They were going swimming together and everything was all right. When the dishes were done, Lucy curled up on the sofa to read, and Carl took the garbage out. When the wind hit him suddenly, he leaned against the railings and, to his own amazement, wept.

He was at the pool by twenty past three and she was already swimming laps. Bleak light glared through the window. When she lifted her head to the side, performing her slow, determined crawl, her eyes were albino.

Carl played in the water; did surface dives, stood on his head in the shallow end. He jackknifed from the low board and he and Lucy swam four laps of side stroke together. Then they dove from opposite sides of the pool, met in the middle, and kissed underwater. They held hands and floated. Finally Carl got out, sat on the side, and watched. She was not swimming for fun or exercise or habit. She had never joined a swimming team, not even in high school. It was like the air for her: she was amphibious.

She got out and sat beside him. Her feet were long and blade-like.

"That was refreshing," he said.

"It's really all right, for a pool."

"If it ever gets warm again, we can swim in Lake Michigan."

"That's the ticket," Lucy said. "It's wonderful in the lake. I was in a couple of weeks ago."

Whatever spell had been broken re-formed. A couple of weeks ago, it had still been winter. She had been swimming out of doors —something unusual enough to tell him about, yet she had seen fit to conceal it. The skin around her nails was grainy and her hair was flat against her head. Drops ran from her bangs to her nose and down her cheeks. He stared at their separate feet, spookily luminescent in the blue water.

The weather got warm and the spring air was sweet. Riders appeared on the bridle paths in Jackson Park. The ground was fuzzy with new grass.

Carl walked under a little stone bridge in the park, listening to the traffic above him. He followed a winding cement path until he came to the rocks that lined the lake. The sun was setting and when the park lights came on, there were halos of mist around them. He climbed the rock steps down to the lake and sat by the water. He had come directly from the office and was still wearing his tie and jacket. Lucy might be home, or she might be on the other side of the park, swimming while he sat. He looked down into the deep water that had contained her and saw mossy algae moving gently with the current. He took off one shoe and sock and tested the water with his toes. It was icy cold. He stretched out on the rocks and watched the sun go down.

It was dark when he got home. Lucy had left a note that she had gone to do some last-minute shopping. His bones felt light and he took a nap on the couch with the windows wide open, and dreamed that he had a fever. He was awakened by Lucy's cool hand on his forehead. In her other hand she was holding a brandy snifter full of water.

"Look," she said. "Snails." In the bottom of the glass were some small stones covered with algae. Two snails sat on the stones, and four clung to the side. The water magnified them, and when he took one out it was gray and tiny in his hand.

"I got them today," she said. "They're all over the rocks. I went snorkeling."

They had a quiet dinner, read the papers, and listened to the Mozart clarinet concerto. Every window was open, and the sweet air breathed in.

Late at night, the bedroom was cool. Lucy slept without a sound, but Carl was awake. He had his arm around her and he put his cheek next to her damp hair. Her sides, as always, were cold, as if under her skin her bones were cold. He watched her sleep and knew that even with his arms around her, she was dreaming in private. He kissed the top of her head, resting his chin on her hair. It gave up a heavy, slightly burned smell: she was drying. A cool lock of hair fell across his wrist and he moved closer to her. In a few weeks, it would be warm enough for them to swim together. Then it would be summer. They would go to Stone Boy Lake and swim some more. It seemed to him that he had done some fine adjusting. What had grieved him was simply a fact: every day of her life she would be at some point damp, then drying, and for one solid time, wet.

the big plum

It was Pineapple Week at the Big Plum supermarket. The checkers wore large straw hats with plastic pineapples affixed to their brims. Binnie Chester, who did not wear a hat, was taping a cutout of a pineapple in evening dress to her cash register at counter three. Harry Markham, whose family owned the Big Plum chain, sat in his manager's booth and watched Binnie Chester as she taped. Each of her gestures contained for him an ultimate purity. Harry noticed these things: at night, after work, he was finishing his dissertation entitled *Vermeer and the Art of the Impossible*. Soon, he would be the only member of the Big Plum staff, including the members of the board —perhaps the only person in the supermarket business—with a Ph.D. in art history. Harry's father often said that when the dissertation was published, they would have a Vermeer Week at the Big Plum, and sell copies of Harry's book on special.

Binnie Chester had spidery fingers with eggshaped nails. Her fine brown hair was coiled into two perfect ovals at the back of her head. Pinned to the front of her Big Plum smock was a plastic plaque that had CHESTER embossed in black letters, and she seemed to be self-conscious about it. From his manager's booth between aisle four, soaps and cleansers, and aisle five, beans and soup, Harry watched Binnie. In his mind, he referred to her as the

Miracle of Rare Device. She cracked gum authoritatively, and when the supermarket was quiet, Harry could hear it. He had discovered that if he hummed the first movement of the Boccherini cello concerto, she was generally on beat. He wondered what she was cracking time to.

She was the only checker Harry didn't know. He was too dazzled to say good morning, and they had never spoken. Looking over the cash registers, he watched seven heads as they bobbed up and down, pushing the change buttons. Butch, at counter one, had dropped out of high school and stole a six-pack of beer every three days. He had worn the same pair of red trousers for eight months. Arleen Solidark, stiffly peruked, extended her bosom over counter two. She had daggerlike nails that were painted a silvery peach. Harry knew that her husband was allergic to cats. Binnie, whose head never bobbed, graced counter three. At counter four was Murray, Harry's cousin, although it was not known at the Big Plum that this relationship existed. He had been thrown out of college for taking drugs. His only substantial facial feature was a mustache, which was known around the counters as "Murray's shredded wheat." Counter five was manned by a rotating series of girls from the local secretarial high school. Mostly they were thick-set and straight-haired, and joked around with Butch. Their names were Trudy, Maryann, and Mary Jo. The sixth and seventh counters belonged to Max and Charlie, both of them old Big Plummers. They were bald and wore glasses. At the end of every day, Max and Charlie did a vaudeville turn around their counters, with brooms.

Harry spent his days fixated on Binnie Chester. She never seemed to speak to anyone, and Harry never saw anyone speak to her. She arrived on time, and left on time, like a European train. After she totaled her receipts at the end of the day, she hung up her Big Plum smock and disappeared. For several months Harry had been planning a collision with her. It would happen at the door, he imagined, and he would ask her out for dinner. He had spent a long time trying to figure out who she was and where she came from, and he had fantasized that she lived in Brooklyn, in an old house of ruined elegance, which had thin lace curtains. Binnie's father, he imagined, was a tall, rakish man with Edwardian sideburns and no job, which accounted for his daughter's working at the Big Plum. There was a grandmother, too, a faded, shapeless woman who gazed blankly, but tragically, out the window. She drank quite a lot of tea. Binnie had several brothers, but Harry hadn't bothered much with them. They looked, he felt, like cleaner editions of Butch. In Harry's fantasy, there was no Binnie's mother. She had died in some way he had not yet worked out. This made him feel protective and tender about Binnie, and he dwelt on her family life as he watched her during the day.

Binnie was looking at the clock. It was nearly closing time. Harry stepped down from his manager's booth and hung up his Big Plum jacket. He straightened his tie, and put on the jacket to his suit. It was his Parisian suit, chocolate brown, and he had worn it because today was Binnie day.

He found her at the streetlight in front of the Big Plum. It was a wet winter night, and she was wearing a wool scarf.

"Excuse me," Harry said. "Miss Chester." Binnie turned around. A circle of streetlight hit her in the face. She was lit like a Vermeer, Harry thought, suddenly feeling inappropriate, explosive, and hysterical. "Um," he said, trying to get his bearings. "You look like a picture in the Frick, a museum, that is. Um, do you know a Dutch painter called Vermeer? You look like one of his pictures." Harry stopped suddenly. Binnie looked patiently at him, as if he were an unfinished card trick.

Then she said, "You're Harry Big Plum."

"Markham," said Harry. "Harry Markham."

"Of the Big Plum," said Binnie.

"I'm the manager," said Harry.

"You're the owner's son," said Binnie.

"That's not generally known," said Harry.

"You think," said Binnie. "And Murray is your cousin."

"That's not known at all."

"Huh," said Binnie, with a little snort. She looked at Harry, who was swaying slightly. He had thick black hair that waved, and large blue eyes that seemed slightly fevered.

"Well, Harry Big Plum," she said. "Why are you swaying around like that and what do you want?"

"I want to walk you home to Brooklyn," said Harry.

"Oh," said Binnie. "I see. Do you live in Brooklyn?"

"No."

"Is there any particular reason why you want to walk from Manhattan to Brooklyn in the cold?"

"Well, I just thought you might live in Brooklyn."

"I don't, though," said Binnie.

"Where do you live?" Harry said.

"Around the corner."

"With your father?"

"My father lives in Minneapolis, with my mother."

"And your grandmother?"

"What grandmother?"

Harry felt close to tears. "I just thought you might have a grandmother," he said, staring at the pavement.

"I see," said Binnie. "I don't have any grandparents at all."

"I'm sorry," said Harry.

"Oh, it's all right. They died when I was very young, and you seem to have come up with replacements."

Harry looked at her. "Are you making fun of me?"

"Listen, Big Plum Markham. You follow me out of your father's store and tell me I live in Brooklyn with my father and grandmother, and then you ask *me* if I'm making fun of *you?*"

"I don't know what to say," mumbled Harry. "I'm awfully sorry. I thought . . ."

"What *did* you think?" asked Binnie. "I'd be very interested to know."

"Look, I'll try to be honest. I mean, I stare at you all day, and I sort of made up this family for you. Look, I'm freezing."

"Start walking," said Binnie. "My home in Brooklyn is just around the corner, and I'll get Granny to fix you a cup of tea."

Harry blushed.

"About my father," said Binnie.

"Really, this is very silly."

"Talk."

"Well, I had this picture of your father as a sort of Edwardian roué, with sideburns and all, and he doesn't work or anything. That's why you work in the Big Plum. And you don't have a mother. This grandmother lives with you. She drinks a lot of tea." He was profoundly embarrassed.

"That's very interesting," said Binnie. "Have you considered a career in fiction?"

Binnie lived on the third floor of a brownstone. Her apartment was painted white, and there was very little in it. Nothing was tacked or hung on the wall. There were no plants, or rugs. She had a sofa made of wooden planks covered with colorless sharkskin pillows and three straight-backed chairs of bleached pine. There was a desk, made out of a whitewashed door. Her bedroom contained a bed with a blue spread, and nothing else. There was a white kitchen with an unpainted table.

"Sit down," said Binnie. "Take off your coat."

"Where should I sit?" asked Harry.

"Any place."

"You don't seem to have much in the way of furniture in here."

"My Edwardian father took it all away," said Binnie, sliding a chair out from under the table.

Harry sat, and put his grubby book bag on the floor. It contained several pamphlets on Vermeer that he needed for his dissertation.

"I guess I got you all wrong," Harry said.

"I guess you did," said Binnie. "How do you want your tea?"

"Milk," said Harry, "and a little sugar." She led him into the living room and he sat on the sofa with his cup. Binnie sat at the desk that was made out of a door.

"Well," said Harry.

"Well what?"

"Tell me how I was wrong."

"You can see how you were wrong."

"I mean," said Harry, "where are you from?"

Binnie unhooked the ovals at the back of her head. Two coils of hair spread over her shoulder.

"My father is a spy and my mother is a zookeeper. My granny teaches Anglo-Saxon at the University of Uruguay," she said, without inflection.

Harry watched her from the sofa. She looked like *The Girl with the Pearl Earrings*. It made him sad to look at her. He felt sullied, and ridiculous. What he wanted to do was suddenly to blurt out the truth to her—the truth about everything: his dissertation, how Murray had been thrown out of school for taking drugs, how he sometimes seemed near to tears in museums, how he watched her, how he felt that she must hate him for being such a fool. The words piled up in the back of his throat, but looking at her cool, uninterrupted face, he began to edit.

"I want to know who you are," he said.

Binnie crossed her legs and leaned back in her chair. "No, you don't, if you really think about it. Aren't you sad that I don't live in some old house in Brooklyn with my granny?"

"No," said Harry sadly. "That was only because I didn't know who you were."

"You still don't," said Binnie, "and tomorrow you can make up a whole new life for me, can't you?"

"As long as I've been so ridiculous," Harry said, "can I ask you another ridiculous question?"

"Sure."

"Do you have any pearl earrings in the shape of a pear, a sort of round pear?"

"No," said Binnie.

"Because," Harry said. "There's a painting of a girl who looks like you, and she has on earrings like that."

"Sorry," said Binnie, pinning her hair back into its ovals.

"I guess I'll go, then. Thank you for the tea. May I see you again?"

Binnie helped him on with his coat. "Sure," she said. "Tomorrow, counter three."

Harry coughed as he walked into his apartment. He had walked all the way home, sixty-five city blocks, so distracted that when he got to his door he reached for his wallet, thinking he had taken a cab. He switched on the light, and sat in his tapestry armchair, under the mobile, and stared at his potted trees. Amidst some hanging plants were reproductions of Vermeer. Over his navy sofa was a real Redon. He had a Persian rug on the floor. Hanging over his bed was what his father called the "Big Plum's Big Plum." It was a painting of Delf Harbor, done by a master of the time of Vermeer. It was his graduation from college present.

Harry sat in his chair and flexed his foot. When he thought of Binnie's empty apartment, the density of his possessions unhinged him. He thought of her unhooking the ovals of her hair, and crossing her legs. He went over every scrap of the conversation between them and came up with something almost as empty as her apartment. He thought how sparse her life was, how tidy and bare. Maybe, he thought, she was someone fleeing from an apartment like his, a rich girl disgusted by possessions, who in rebellion had stocked her house with nothing, and worked as a supermarket checker out of spite. It seemed to fit her, he thought, raging against a father who was perhaps an art historian and a cultivated mother, a house full of Meissen and a couple of Caravaggios.

He sighed, and went to his writing table. On a clean sheet of paper, he wrote:

CADENCE IN VERMEER

Cadence is not a term often applied to painting. I use it here to infer the way in which light becomes, not color, but an entity in itself.

Consider cadence as the way in which a slot or neighborhood of color sweeps from an intensity of power to an apex which is in fact less or more brilliant than that of its beginning. Light in the works of Vermeer has nothing to do with the placement of color. For the first time, light is something other than color. Something which has, in fact, nothing to do with painting.

Harry stopped, and thought of Binnie. He traveled over her in his mind, as if he were in his manager's perch, looking down to her. Watching her tie up the cash register for the evening always made him melancholy, and he was melancholy thinking about it now. He felt like a man in a Rembrandt, tinged brown with sorrow and wisdom.

He looked at his dissertation, or the heap that was to become his dissertation, and sighed again. He was of two minds about this Vermeer business, and he was of two minds about this supermarket business. That accounted for four minds in all, and it made life painful for him. During the day, his thesis gnawed at him, but when he sat down to write it, he remembered that two cases of ginger ale had arrived frozen, that the Camembert was being returned because it was overripe, and that after weeks of trying out Humbolt's new pork and beans with pickles, none of the five cases had been sold. During the day, he dreamed at his manager's perch of a supermarket that looked like the Sistine chapel: fruit hung in porcelain baskets. He dreamed of Vermeer brand tomato paste. Binnie wandered through this supermarket in an embroidered robe. The cash register was mother of pearl. Often, her face appeared on the label for Vermeer brand peaches. Her cash register spat out totals on a little flag of silk. He felt a little gong of sadness go off in his head, and he fell asleep at his desk with his jacket on.

Harry sat at his manager's perch, tallying up receipts for orange juice. It was a fresh new day. Often he felt noble sitting there, as if he brought a higher wisdom to the store, but he knew he didn't: Max and Charlie knew more about packing, shipping, bills of lading, price fixing, and where to get the best fennel than he did. But Harry's father often said that the real sign a family had become established was when it produced an intellectual, and Harry was it. Still, Harry often thought that he was compelled by this attitude of his father's to feel noble, when what he really felt was dreamy, transfixed, tired, and stricken. The sum total of his day's work seemed to be hours of staring at Binnie Chester, and trying to get the coffee shipments coordinated at the same time. It was good for Harry, Harry's father had told him, to work at the Big Plum—all the Markhams had worked there. It was good for his dissertation, Harry's father said, because it is good for the intellectually inclined to see what the real world is like, the world of people like Max and Charlie, and Butch and Arleen Solidark. Besides, Harry's father maintained, working in trade would give him a thirst for art, so that when Harry went home at night, he would go to his dissertation as a starving man goes to a banquet.

The day began when Binnie walked in. It was overcast and a pale, pearly light shone down on the rows of bottles, tins, cans, and boxes. Even the packages of detergent had a sheen to them. Binnie slipped quietly behind counter three and tied on her Big Plum smock. When she leaned over to check the stack of shopping bags, Harry noticed that she moved like someone who had been to ballet school. He imagined her in Minneapolis—Minneapolis to him was large and open, like a room at the Hermitage in Leningrad, white-walled with scrolled moldings. Outside lay a flat stretch of snow, and some very green pine trees. In this room in Minneapolis was Binnie, dressed in a pale leotard, exercising at the barre. She was driven to her ballet classes by a chauffeur who arranged a plaid rug over her knees. It was very cold in Minneapolis. She was all alone in this wide room, doing spins and pirouettes.

He caught her at the door at closing time.

"Have you ever taken ballet lessons?"

Binnie looked up at him. When he saw her face, he wanted to turn away. Her mouth curved down at the corners, and her eyes were tired. She looked as if she were in pain.

"Look," she said slowly. "Enough's enough. Leave me alone with all this. Go write a novel about ballet in the A&P." She bunched her scarf around her neck and ran, a little knock-kneed, around the corner and out of sight.

Murray, Harry's cousin, was supposed to be learning a sense of responsibility at the Big Plum.

"I'm putting in time here, man," he said to Harry. "So are you."

"It's good for my dissertation," said Harry. "It's the principle of opposites."

"What the hell does that mean?" said Murray.

"It means that the supermarket business has nothing to do with art history or Vermeer, but that the conditions I face every day, which are antithetical to my thesis, put a pressure on me to get it done, see?"

"No," said Murray.

"I don't know how they let you into college, Murray," Harry said.

"They threw me out, man," said Murray.

It was the fifth day since Binnie had run away from him at the corner of the Big Plum. She was as impassive as an apple; she barely looked at the customers as she rang up their carts of groceries. Harry looked down at her from his manager's perch, staring at her sadly. He felt like a vegetable without its skin: raw and vulnerable. Often he thought he would cry. Once he did, over a green order form. Tears slid down his face, and he was glad that he was alone in his manager's perch, glad that he was bent over so that no one could see him. He brooded over Binnie, over his dissertation, and over Murray, who had been late every morning for a week. He had been told to get Murray in line.

He took Murray out to lunch. Around the corner from the Big Plum was a small, gritty Italian restaurant where they had a plate of clams each.

"Now, look Murray," Harry began.

"Yeah, look what," said Murray.

"Well, for starters you don't come in on time, and second they don't think you're performing."

"Yeah, yeah," said Murray, stabbing a clam with the tip of his fork.

"You have to listen," said Harry.

"Oh, man. What a drag," whined Murray. "You listen. You come in on time, but you don't even do anything except sit around and cry and look at Binnie."

"Cry?" shouted Harry. "Binnie?"

"Yeah, yeah." Murray stared at his cousin with his glazed eyes. "I may come into work stoned, man, but I have an appreciation of reality."

"Reality?" Harry said softly.

"This Binnie business is out of hand," said Murray.

"What Binnie business?"

"Man, I got eyes. You sit up there on that cat perch and stare. I can see it."

"Who knows about this, Murray?"

"There's nothing to know except you stare."

"Murray," said Harry, leaning over his clams. "What do you know about her?"

"Nothing," said Murray. "She's a nice broad."

Harry cornered Binnie in front of her house.

"Why, it's the Big Plum," she said evenly.

"Did you ever think that it's not fair to know about me when I don't know about you?" Harry asked.

"No," said Binnie.

"You have to tell me. Why won't you say who you are."

"You know who I am. It says so on my smock. Binnie Chester."

"But look, why are you working there? You're not like the other checkers."

"Maybe I was thrown out of college for drugs like Murray."

"No one knows about that," said Harry.

"You think," said Binnie. "What are you doing there? What's Murray doing there?"

"Murray's there to learn a sense of responsibility, and I'm there because it's the antithesis of my dissertation, and it's good for me to know another side of life."

"I see," said Binnie. "Well, I work there because I like it."

"Because you *like* it?" Harry asked.

"You own the place," said Binnie. "Don't you think it's a fit place for people to work?"

"I . . . I guess so," said Harry lamely. Binnie looked at Harry. There was nothing in her face that wasn't serious. She looked and saw that his eyes were ultramarine blue, and that they were stricken.

"I'll give you a cup of tea," she said.

Binnie drank her tea at the desk made out of a door. Harry sat on the sofa.

"You like this sort of thing, don't you?" Binnie said.

"What sort of thing?" asked Harry.

"Fitting little details together until you have a nice tidy picture."

"I'm sort of an art historian," mumbled Harry.

"In your case," said Binnie, "that has nothing to do with life."

"I just wanted to know . . ."

"I *know* what you wanted to know," said Binnie. "And now I'm going to tell you. I'm twenty-five. I come from Minneapolis. My father is a foreman in a lumber yard and my mother is a housewife. I used to be a checker in the Safeway in Minneapolis. Now I'm here."

"Is that true?" Harry asked.

"It's the first version," said Binnie. "Here's the second. I'm twenty-five, from Minneapolis. My father is a mathematician and my mother is a doctor. I went to the University of Chicago and did European history. Now I work at your Big Plum because it's the only thing I can stand. Choose the one you want. Either will help you out."

"Help me out?" whispered Harry.

"Now you know what you wanted to know, Big Plum. And you even get your choice of flavors. Now take the one you want and finish your little dissertation about yourself."

"I don't understand," said Harry.

"Of course you don't," said Binnie. She smiled. Then she

stopped smiling. "You don't even know when enough's enough. You don't even know who not to begin with."

"What am I supposed to believe, then? About you, I mean."

"Whichever suits you. It's your dissertation. Have both. It has nothing to do with me, anyway." She got up from her chair, did an abrupt dancer's turn, and opened the door for him. "I'm very serious," she said.

"Serious about what?" Harry asked.

"Everything," said Binnie, holding out his coat like a sign.

"I'll see you tomorrow," mumbled Harry into his collar.

On the street, Harry felt as if he had spilled a large pot of tar on the Unicorn tapestry. He felt like the Florence flood. In the beginning he had thought he was just after a nice young girl so he could take her out to dinner, but it wasn't so. Binnie knew it wasn't so. It's your dissertation, she had said. He wondered what she meant. He wondered what he did want to know, and why, and why so much.

He walked in large, haphazard patterns toward his apartment, away from it, toward Binnie's, and back toward home. There was no letup. She hadn't told him anything at all.